Under Crook's Wood

A.B. Martin

Cover design by Books Covered.
Formatting by Polgarus Studio

www.abmartinauthor.com

For Beatrice
With all my love

CHAPTER 1

'There are dark powers in this wood,' said Daniel, glancing towards the trees, 'spirits of the night that can play tricks on your mind and change your life forever.'

It was mid-October, and the pale evening sun flickered through the tops of the trees as the last few rays of light cast their dim shadows to the ground. In a clearing in Crook's Wood, on the outskirts of town, a group of teenagers were larking about in the twilight, entertaining themselves with stories of ghosts and monstrous creatures of terror.

They were gathered around two picnic tables, the girls all huddled together for warmth, as the temperature dropped and the colour drained out of the day. This was where the people of the town went in the summer to get close to nature and give their children a chance to run free, safe from the roar of the traffic. There were picnic tables and a parking area, and on hot days an ice cream van would park close by to tempt the little ones to badger their parents to buy. But in the evening it was a favourite haunt of the local teenagers and tonight Daniel Fletcher was the chief storyteller.

'Tread carefully if you enter this wood,' said Daniel, widening his eyes theatrically. 'At the end of the day, as the light begins to fade, strange and mysterious things can occur. A primeval force emerges from the shadows and the wood becomes a very different place.'

He paused and glanced towards the trees for dramatic effect.

'There are spectres and spirits here, and weird things happen that no one has ever been able to explain. The strange mists that appear and cause people to lose track of time, the mysterious circle of earth where nothing will grow and animals refuse to enter, and the sightings of the headless oarsman, rowing across the lake, that fade and disappear on reaching the trees at the other side.'

The others stared at him in silence, occasionally glancing towards the trees apprehensively. The wood looked dark and sinister and Grace, the youngest of the girls, was starting to become increasingly uncomfortable. She felt as if the trees were watching her, waiting for the right moment to swallow her up. Shifting anxiously in her seat, she took a deep breath and looked around at the others for reassurance.

But not everyone was convinced by Daniel's theatrics. One lone sceptic refused to be drawn into the mounting mood of terror.

'That's a load of superstitious nonsense,' said Matt, clearly looking to impress the girls who were gathered together on one table. He leaned back and shook his head dismissively.

'Oh yeah?' said Daniel. 'That's what Tom Franklin thought when he accepted a dare to spend a night alone in the wood. But he wasn't laughing when they found him the following morning, was he?'

'Why, what happened to him?' asked Grace, not really wanting to hear the answer.

Daniel paused once again and slowly moved his gaze around the group. He was enjoying parading around, telling his ghoulish stories, and he wasn't going to let Matt's scepticism knock him off his stride.

'It was a full moon,' he continued, glancing up at the sky, 'but the clouds made sure no light penetrated the canopy of the trees as Tom left his friends and strode into the heart of the wood. At first it seemed such a peaceful place, the perfect spot for him to gather his thoughts and find a little stillness. The serenity didn't last though. Soon he heard the sound of heavy footsteps, and he knew that he wasn't alone.

He laughed and sat down on a log, thinking his friends had crept into the wood to try to unnerve him. But then he saw the creature's red satanic eyes and heard its low growl as it slowly circled him, waiting for the moment to strike. Nobody but the trees heard his terrified screams or witnessed what occurred that night, but by morning Tom Franklin was not the same person. The creature had taken his soul and Tom was now an empty shell, a shadow of the man he could have been.'

The others sat and listened intently, occasionally glancing nervously towards the trees and the darkness that lay beyond them.

'It's in there now,' said Daniel, 'waiting for the next naive traveller to happen along. Who knows, perhaps it's watching us at this very moment, waiting to make its move.'

Once again he paused, trying to use the stillness to add a little tension to the end of his story.

'What a load of old twaddle that was, Fletcher,' said Matt, defiantly puncturing the mood.

Grace bit her lip and pulled her jacket more tightly around her shoulders.

'Did you make all that up, Daniel?' she asked.

'Of course he did,' said Matt. 'We've all lived in this town for most of our lives. If there really was something evil living in this wood don't you think we'd have heard about it before now?'

But Grace wasn't so sure. She fidgeted with her hair and looked nervously across at the trees.

'I don't like it up here,' she said. 'Let's go back to the town.'

She stood up and gathered her things together, hoping the other girls would follow suit.

'What was that?' said Emily.

'What was what?' Matt answered.

'I heard something in the wood. Listen.'

At first everything was quiet, but after a few seconds it happened again. They heard the sound of a branch breaking and of heavy feet shuffling through the undergrowth.

'What's going on in there?' said Grace, looking at Daniel and Matt.

'Oh, it's probably a demonic squirrel waiting to contaminate us all and turn us into nut gatherers,' said Matt, grinning at her.

'Don't mess around, Matt,' said Emily, 'can't you see that she's frightened?'

'Maybe you should go and investigate, Matt,' said Daniel, seeking to regain the upper hand.

'OK,' said Matt, 'I think I will. If I'm not back in ten minutes call the squirrel rescue squad. And tell them to bring nuts. They may be after a ransom.'

He stood up and walked off towards the darkness of the wood, chuckling to himself and strutting with exaggerated bravado. The others sat in silence and watched him disappear into the trees.

'Is that story really true, Daniel?' said Emily. 'Or is it just another one of your attempts to spook us all out?'

'Who knows what's true and what isn't?' said Daniel, with great dramatic effect.

Grace didn't care whether it was true or not. After hearing those sounds in the wood she just wanted to get right away from there.

'Are we waiting for him then?' she said, looking at the other girls but obviously wanting to leave straight away. It was starting to get dark, and she felt unnerved by the spookiness of the area. She craved the predictability and certainty of the town, and she wished Matt hadn't gone to investigate.

A few minutes passed.

'Do you think he's alright in there?' said Emily, looking across at Daniel. 'He's been gone for quite a while.'

They didn't have to wait long to get their answer. A scream of terror pierced the air and they all looked at one another nervously.

'It's just Matt messing around,' said Daniel, trying to give the others a bit of comfort. 'He's probably watching us right now, hoping we'll all freak out and start running back towards the town.'

But he couldn't have been more wrong. Seconds later, Matt burst from the wood running for all he was worth. His jacket was ripped at the shoulder and there was a graze on the side of his face.

'Run!' he shouted, charging towards them at speed. 'Get out of here, now!'

His eyes were wide with terror and he seemed to be in a blind panic, but the others still weren't sure whether this was all a ruse to get them to become hysterical and stampede into the town. Then they saw the creature.

At first it was just a dark shape moving through the trees, but when they caught a brief glimpse of its face they knew this wasn't a joke. Its demonic red eyes exuded menace and evil. They were trespassing on its territory and it wanted them gone.

Daniel stood there open-mouthed as Matt and the others charged off down the hill towards the town. Could he possibly have conjured up this creature through the force of his imagination? Was he really that powerful?

He caught a fleeting glimpse of a monstrous hairy figure moving through the trees to his left. For such a colossal beast, it seemed to move with tremendous speed. He stood and gazed at it in amazement, caught between awe and terror, but when the creature let out a chilling howl of anger it was enough to bring him back to reality. He turned and ran, following his friends down the hill, desperate to get back to the safety of the town.

When they burst into the police station to report what they had seen, the police were a little sceptical from the word go. They had been the victims of hoaxes and pranks by teenagers in the past and this sounded just as unlikely.

'This is Hampton Spa, not Transylvania,' said the desk sergeant. 'I think you kids have been watching too many horror movies. You don't get monsters in the Weald of Kent.'

The following day the police made a full search of the wood but there was no trace of the creature anywhere, and when the investigating officers returned to the town they filed their notes under 'Monster in Crook's Wood' and promptly closed the case.

CHAPTER 2

'You're going to blow this town apart next Thursday,' said Sophie, following her mum into the kitchen and settling herself down at the table. 'It's going to be such a brilliant night. I am so looking forward to it.'

'Thank you darling,' said Mrs Watson, 'but let's not count our chickens just yet. There's still a long way to go and anything could happen.'

But Sophie's enthusiasm was unstoppable.

'Well, now the half-term holiday has started, and I've got a week off school, I'm happy to help out in any way I can. You're going to storm this election Mum, I just know you are.'

It was breakfast time in the Watson household and Mrs Watson had been up for ages, preparing for the day and answering the tons of emails and texts she had received overnight. As the Green Party's candidate for

Hampton Spa, she was determined to make every second count in the final days before next week's general election. All the main political parties believed they were in with a chance of winning the local seat. In fact, it was so close that the Prime Minister himself was due to visit Hampton Spa in a few days time. The whole town was buzzing with anticipation and Sophie was her mum's biggest cheerleader.

'And I'm so glad that Sienna's going to be here for Election Day,' said Sophie, still buzzing with energy. 'She'll be able to join in the celebrations when you win. This is going to be so awesome.'

Sophie had been looking forward to this week for quite some time and, now it had finally arrived, the excitement was bubbling over inside her. Not only did she have the thrill of the election, and a whole week off school, but her friend Sienna was due to arrive on Tuesday and would be staying for several days. It was the first time the girls had seen one another since the summer, and Sophie was so excited about Sienna's visit she could barely contain herself.

An image flashed into her mind of the moment she and Sienna first met. Sophie was staying at her Uncle John's hotel in Bramlington Bay, on the Dorset coast, and while he was showing her around some empty rooms on the top floor Sienna made quite a dramatic entrance, manifesting out of thin air after travelling through a portal from another world.

At sixteen years of age, she was the youngest member of The Elite, a covert security force on a parallel world called Galacdros, and she was on the trail of Osorio, a dissident fugitive who had stolen a precious stone called The Orb of Nendaro.

Sienna was daring and fearless and driven by a desire for truth and justice and, over the next few days, as Sophie got to know her, the girls quickly developed a solid friendship. It was this close bond that had given them the edge when they were caught up in a life or death struggle on mysterious Kestrel Island.

They had gone out to the island in search of Osorio, determined to recover The Orb. In the process they discovered an evil plan to develop mind control drugs and a plot to take over the British government. Somehow they managed to disrupt the plan and survive Osorio's murderous attempts to make them pay with their lives, but being chased across the island by armed killers and staring down the barrel of a gun, believing she was about to die, had changed Sophie forever.

She still had nightmares about that harrowing time, and Osorio, the power-crazed fugitive they had gone to the island to find, was still at large. He could be anywhere by now and Sophie knew that he was bound to be seeking revenge.

She reached up instinctively to touch her arm, remembering the bullet that had ripped through her sleeve as they fled into the night. She had been lucky. The wound was only skin deep. Another few inches to the side and it could have ripped through her heart.

In the days and weeks that followed their ordeal Sophie had resolved to become just as powerful and courageous as her friend. Despite being only twelve years old and of a slighter build than Sienna, she was determined to make the best of what she had.

Initially, it wasn't easy. In her first few karate lessons she felt awkward and clumsy, and her early attempts to go out for a run left her breathless and spent. But as the weeks rolled into months her confidence and strength improved enormously, and she was now beginning to reap the benefits of all her hard work.

The door to the kitchen swung open and Sophie's Dad entered the room, smiling broadly and carrying a copy of the local newspaper.

'Good morning darling,' he said, bending down to kiss Sophie on the top of the head. 'Have you had any breakfast yet?'

'Erm, no,' she replied. 'I'll probably grab something when we get into town.'

Sophie had volunteered to help her mum in the town that morning, and she was hoping to get something sweet and tasty from one of the local coffee shops.

'Would you like me to put some toast on?' Mr Watson asked.

'No, I think you should wear your regular clothes,' said Sophie, smiling at him. 'You wouldn't look good wearing toast.'

'Oh yes, very funny,' said Mr Watson, settling down to read the newspaper. He studied it for several seconds then gave a quiet chuckle.

'I see the local students have been up to their old tricks again,' he said, holding up the front page.

The newspaper carried the headline "Terror in Crook's Wood" and underneath was an artist's impression of the terrifying creature that was said to have made an attack on some teenagers earlier in the week.

'Apparently, some teenagers were attacked by a

monster up by Crook's Wood the other night,' said Mr Watson. 'If you ask me it was probably students messing around with a Halloween costume.'

Sophie studied the drawing of the creature on the front page of the newspaper.

'It looks a bit like Chewbacca from Star Wars,' she said, shaking her head and smiling.

'Well, it wasn't much of a laugh for the people who saw it,' said Mr Watson. 'According to this article, they're all lucky to be alive. Look at this. Turn to page five for a full account from eyewitness Daniel Fletcher.'

'Oh no,' said Sophie. 'Not Daniel Fletcher. If he's involved it's bound to be a hoax.'

'Do you know him then?'

'He's in year eleven at our school and he's always up to something. You think he could have dreamt up a scarier looking monster than that though.'

Sophie's mum had been sitting at the table, oblivious to the conversation that was going on around her. She finished thumbing in the umpteenth text she'd sent that morning, drained her coffee cup, then stood up and put her coat on.

'Maybe you should get Chewbacca to campaign for the Green Party darling,' said Mr Watson, holding up the drawing of the creature. 'I mean, if he came knocking at your door and asked for your vote you'd think twice about saying no.'

'Yes, thank you dear,' she said, smiling at him. 'And you wonder why I don't take you out on the campaign trail with me.'

Mr Watson chuckled and studied the front page again then he turned to Sophie looking a little concerned.

'Don't you normally go for a run up by Crook's Wood?' he asked.

'Yes, I do,' Sophie answered, putting on her jacket. 'And if I see Chewbacca up there I'll let you know. Although looking at that drawing, I'd be very surprised if he could find a pair of running shoes in his size.'

It was a busy Saturday morning in central Hampton Spa. The town was alive with weekend shoppers, and Mrs Watson had to drive around for ages before she could find somewhere to park. Finally they found a spot, just off the high street, and she reversed the car carefully into the tiny space. It was metered parking and she was sure it was going to cost the earth, but at least they were still quite close to the shopping mall.

She leaned back in her seat and breathed a sigh of relief, but her moment of joy was short lived. When she stepped out of the car she found herself face to face with an old adversary. Will Starkey, a journalist for a national newspaper, who had written an article earlier in the year attacking Mrs Watson and The Green Party.

'Not cycling into town to save the planet?' said Starkey. 'One law for you and another for everyone else is it?'

'How I travel around is none of your business,' said Mrs Watson, pushing a series of coins into the parking meter.

'Well, I think it is my business if your bogus party keeps telling us that our cars are polluting the world but it's still OK for you to drive into the town. What's the matter? Is the bus not good enough for you? That's the trouble with you environmental loonies, as soon as it's inconvenient for you to make any effort you forget all about the environment.'

Mrs Watson ignored him. She opened the back door of the car and handed a box of leaflets to Sophie.

'And I see you've brought a young slave along to do all your heavy lifting,' Starkey continued.

'If you must know this is my daughter,' said Mrs

Watson. 'And Sophie darling, this creature is an example of how not to end up when you're an adult.'

Sophie didn't need to be told. She had taken an instant dislike to this man. He was shifty and ill-mannered and she couldn't wait to get away from him.

'Anyway,' said Mrs Watson. 'What are you doing in Hampton Spa? I thought you said wild horses couldn't drag you back here.'

'Well, normally they couldn't,' said Starkey. 'But our glorious Prime Minister is paying the town a visit in a few days time and my editor thinks that my local knowledge will be significant.'

'And will it?' said Mrs Watson.

'Only if it's important to know what a nothing kind of a place this is,' said Starkey. 'There isn't enough genuine news in this town to fill a postage stamp. I see the front page of the local paper is trying to convince us there's a monster on the loose in Crook's Wood.'

'Really?' said Mrs Watson. 'I didn't know you spent your evenings wandering around Crook's Wood.'

'Oh, ha, ha, ha,' said Starkey. 'Yes, very funny. Well if I did it would probably be the biggest story to hit this town in decades. Local boy returns to Hampton Spa, remembers what a dump it is and goes mad in Crook's Wood.'

'Maybe it's only a dump when you're here,' said Mrs Watson. 'Perhaps when you leave town the sun comes out and all the flowers burst into bloom in celebration.'

Sophie was enjoying watching her mum taunting this bitter man. She was sparky and witty and seemed to be able to outsmart him, no matter what he said.

'I suppose you'll be meeting him will you?' said Starkey.

'Who do you mean,' said Mrs Watson, 'the Prime Minister or the monster?' She was clearly enjoying poking fun at him.

'Maybe they're the same person,' Starkey answered, trying to introduce some humour himself.

'Well, even if they're not, I'm sure you'll find a way to make it look like they are.'

'Hey, I'll simply be reporting the facts,' said Starkey. 'And I'm not going to be fobbed off either. If he won't give me a straight answer I'm going to follow him around the square until he does.'

'Really?' said Mrs Watson. 'Well, fascinating though all of this is, if you'll excuse us we've got work to do. '

'Work?' said Starkey. 'You've got no chance of winning this election. You'll probably end up with about fifty votes and most of them will be from your family and friends.'

He stood by the car and watched Sophie and her mum as they slowly walked away towards the shopping mall. He hated the Green Party with a passion and he hated Mrs Watson even more. Perhaps it was fate that he was going to be in town for the next few days and would have plenty of time to do a bit of digging around. How deliciously sweet it would be if he could dig up some dirt about Mrs Watson and make absolutely certain her election campaign was a disaster.

'Who was that horrible man?' Sophie asked, as she and her mum made their way towards the shopping mall.

'His name is Will Starkey. He's a journalist for The Daily Press.'

'Well, he gave me the creeps,' said Sophie. 'I did enjoy the way you were mocking him though. It was very funny. '

Mrs Watson smiled then turned and looked intently at Sophie.

'Keep away from him if you see him around the town though, darling,' she said. 'He's a strange man, and I think there's something a bit weird about him.'

CHAPTER 3

With the wind now at her back, Sienna felt a fresh surge of energy. She darted past the beach cafe and sprinted down the coast road, desperate to reach The Grand Hotel before it was too late. Gritting her teeth and straining for an extra yard of speed, she drove herself powerfully forward, her heart pounding in her chest and beads of salty sweat running down her face into her eyes and mouth.

It was now an all out sprint, like an Olympic champion in the home straight, driving herself towards the finish line. Her legs were screaming with the pain of her exertions but there could be no letting up, she had to make it there in time. Failure was not an option.

Still moving at full tilt, she flashed through the entrance gates of the hotel and powered across the gravel car park before collapsing onto the little white bench just outside the door. At last she could look at her watch. Excellent! Another fifteen seconds had been shaved off her fastest time, and she was certain she would soon get even quicker.

The hotel owner, John Hodgson, had been watching her exertions from inside the lobby. He strolled out into the crisp evening air and sat down on the bench beside her.

'Wow,' he said. 'You were really moving at speed there.'

'Yes,' said Sienna, desperately trying to catch her breath. 'That was twenty seven, thirty five, which is fifteen seconds quicker than my previous best. I'm not far away from being back to full fitness now.'

John smiled and nodded his approval. For the last three months he had been watching Sienna trying to rebuild her strength, and he couldn't help admiring her gritty determination. She had been pushing herself to the limit in a gruelling daily workout and her persistence was finally starting to pay off.

To anyone who asked him, Sienna was the teenage daughter of an old friend of the family who was helping out around the hotel while she stayed in the town. But to John she was the girl who had materialised out of thin air one afternoon while he was showing his niece Sophie around the rooms on the top floor. Sienna had travelled through a portal from a parallel world on the trail of a dissident fugitive called Osorio, and John was determined to help her in any way he could. Her father, Memphis, had once saved his life and John was happy to take the chance to return the favour.

Only Sophie and John knew the truth about Sienna, and only John knew what had really happened to the girls during that terrifying night they spent on Kestrel Island. They had both been close to death on more than one occasion, and when he finally caught up with them they were badly dehydrated and Sienna was seriously injured.

It had been a long, slow road to recovery for Sienna after the battering her body had taken. A broken arm, three fractured ribs and extensive bruising down her left hand side, but she knew that she was lucky to be alive. When she was wrestling with Osorio at the top of a cliff, she had no idea they were so close to the edge. She could still picture the look on his face as he lost his footing and tumbled down the cliff face, dragging her over with him to the sand below. Miraculously they had both survived the fall, but when Sienna woke up Osorio was gone and so was The Orb, the prize she had worked so hard to take from him.

John's wife Hannah appeared at the door of the hotel and strolled over to where they were sitting. 'That looked like hard work,' she said. 'You must be ready for something to eat.'

'I will be soon,' Sienna answered. 'I'm going to take a walk along the beach first. I've got some stretching and cool down exercises to do and then I'm going to take a long hot shower.'

The fresh sea breeze felt good on her face as she crossed the coast road and made her way down onto the beach. It was almost deserted apart from an elderly lady who was sitting on a bench a little further down, staring out at the sea.

In the distance, Sienna could see the outline of Kestrel Island silhouetted against the sky. It looked so peaceful on this beautiful October evening, an oasis of calm shimmering on the horizon. Such a stark contrast to the terrifying ordeal the girls had endured that summer. Three months had passed since that desperate night. Three months for her to ruminate on how she had taken The Orb from Osorio only to lose it again. It had been a bitter pill to swallow. On her first mission for The

Elite she had been so close to achieving her goal, yet at the last minute victory had been snatched from her grasp.

The sound of a barking dog brought her mind back to reality. A man threw a stick into the waves, and his bouncy lolloping dog rushed into the sea to retrieve it. Once back on the beach it dropped the stick at the man's feet then shook itself vigorously, drenching the man with the spray. Sienna chuckled at the innocence of the dog's playfulness and continued her walk along the beach.

Soon she was only about twenty feet away from the elderly lady who was sitting on the bench, and now she could see her more clearly she was struck by the woman's stature and demeanour. In contrast to so many elderly people in the town, this woman looked strong and confident. She was immaculately dressed in a dark coat and silk scarf and she wore a hat with a flamboyant looking feather attached with a silver hatpin. As Sienna approached the bench the lady turned and spoke to her.

'Hello Sienna,' she said. 'I was hoping you'd walk down this way again tonight.'

Sienna paused for a moment, wondering how the woman knew her.

'I'm sorry,' she said. 'I'm afraid I don't recognise you.'

'Well, it's been a long time since we last met,' said the woman. 'My name is Jutan. I am a friend of your father's.'

On hearing the woman's name Sienna remembered her immediately. Jutan was a former head of The Elite, in Galacdros, and was once her father's commanding officer. He often spoke of how much he respected Jutan and what a privilege it had been to serve under her.

'Your father is very proud that you have followed him into The Elite,' said Jutan, smiling warmly.

Sienna returned Jutan's smile and sat down on the bench next to her.

'I hope to continue to make him proud,' she said, 'by returning The Orb to its rightful place in the Senate. I had it in my grasp for a while earlier in the summer, but I'm afraid I failed to hold onto it.'

'Don't focus too much on that,' said Jutan, 'your mission isn't over yet.'

'I thought you'd left The Elite,' said Sienna. 'My father told me that you'd retired from the service and moved to the Gonokrian coast.'

'Retirement didn't suit me,' said Jutan. 'My brain

needs to be active, so the Senate gave me a position in this world to advise our agents and liaise with the security forces here.'

Sienna had seen this trait in her father and some of his friends. They were so driven by their careers that when it was time to take a break they didn't know what to do with themselves. Clearly Jutan had missed The Elite even more than the service had missed her.

'How did you know I'd be coming this way?' Sienna asked.

'You've walked on this stretch of the beach every night this week,' Jutan answered. 'If I was a predator, and you were my prey, you would be very easy to track down. I'd just sit on this bench every evening and wait for you to walk past.'

'But I enjoy this part of the beach. It's where I cool down after my workout.'

Jutan smiled at her then turned and looked out to Kestrel Island.

'You and your friend disrupted a very dangerous plan in the summer,' she said. 'If Osorio had successfully developed mind control drugs and taken over the British Government, the world would now have a very uncertain future. A man like Osorio will not let that pass without revenge.'

'Does that mean I should stay off the beach?' said Sienna.

'No, it means you should vary your routines,' Jutan answered. 'Someone may be watching you on behalf of Osorio, and if they can predict your behaviour as easily as I can it makes you vulnerable. You are a member of The Elite. You must be unpredictable, almost invisible.'

Sienna thought about her daily routine. Jutan was right. If anyone was watching her on Osorio's behalf she was a sitting duck.

'Do you know if Osorio is still in this area?' she asked.

'I'm afraid I don't,' said Jutan. 'We know he's being helped by a businessman called James Masterson and is probably staying at one of Masterson's properties in the south of England, but we can't be sure exactly where he is. However, our intelligence suggests that Osorio could have moved his operation to Kent.'

'Kent?' said Sienna, looking a little alarmed. 'That's where my friend Sophie lives.'

'Is she the girl who was with you on Kestrel Island?'

'Yes,' Sienna answered. 'I'm going to see her on Tuesday. I'll be staying in Hampton Spa for a few days while she's off school.'

'Then I must update you with everything we know

about Osorio,' said Jutan, with a look of urgency.

She stood up with the agility of a twenty-year-old.

'Let's walk along the seafront,' she said, 'it will make it easier to talk confidentially.'

As they walked along the promenade deep in conversation, anyone who saw them could have been forgiven for thinking that Sienna was taking an early evening stroll with her very elegant grandmother. They would never have guessed that Jutan used to run the most powerful counter terrorism unit on Galacdros.

Sienna listened intently as Jutan told her all the latest intelligence on Osorio's likely whereabouts. They couldn't be sure of his exact location, but her contacts believed he may be in Kent looking for a Galacdrian scientist called Professor Felso.

'Felso has a brilliant mind,' said Jutan, 'but unfortunately he also has an obsession with his craft.'

'And what is his craft?' Sienna asked.

'He designs and builds incredibly lifelike androids. They look almost like people. You've probably seen the androids that work as security guards at the Senate building in Galacdros. They were all designed by Professor Felso.'

'Wow,' said Sienna. 'They are spookily lifelike. But why is he now living in this world?'

'Well, for years he had been trying to develop androids that contained a basic range of emotions and, as you may know, this is forbidden by Galacdros law. When he continued to flout the rule of law, he was brought up before the Senate and exiled from our world indefinitely. Fortunately for him, the authorities on earth agreed to let him live here provided he was prepared to abandon his work.'

'And has he?' Sienna asked.

'I'm afraid we don't know. And to make matters worse, we're not actually sure where he is anymore. He was last known to be living in Kent but that's as much as we have on him.'

'But why would Osorio be looking for him?'

'We think he may try to persuade Felso to build him an army of androids to assist him in his bid to take power on Galacdros. Those security guards at the Senate are incredibly powerful. If Osorio had a battalion of them under his command it would be very dangerous.'

As they approached the end of the promenade they could hear shouting and laughter coming from a small group of people up ahead. A middle-aged man was sitting on a bench. His clothes were threadbare and grubby and his coat was tied at the waist by a length of rope. It looked as if he had been asleep on the bench and had just been rudely awakened by a loud and aggressive group of young men.

He seemed tormented and trapped, like a cornered fox surrounded by a pack of yapping hounds, desperate to escape but fearful of what might happen if he tried to flee. One of the men poured a can of beer over his head then screwed up the can and threw it at him, laughing as it bounced off his shoulder and fell to the ground.

Jutan was visibly outraged. She stopped and glared at the man who had poured the beer.

'I think this gentleman would prefer to be able to go back to sleep,' she said.

'What's it to you, Grandma?' said the man. 'Is he your boyfriend?'

The other men all burst out laughing as their friend stared arrogantly back at Jutan.

'Look, why don't you and your friends take your high spirits a little further down the beach?' Jutan, answered.

'Or what?' said the man. 'Are you going to make me sit on the naughty step?'

He smiled and looked across at his friends, who were enjoying having a laugh at the old lady's expense, but when he turned back towards Jutan his mood changed quite dramatically. His eyes narrowed and he pulled out a long knife which he held out threateningly in her direction.

'I'll tell you what, Grandma,' he said. 'You hand over that purse of yours and we'll forget about the whole thing.'

The speed and power of Jutan's reaction took Sienna totally by surprise. She shot out her hand and grabbed hold of the back of the man's wrist, twisting it sharply and causing him to drop the knife at her feet. At the same time, she smashed her other elbow into his jaw with such force that he let out a guttural cry of pain and slumped to the ground like a rag doll.

When the other men rushed across to assist their friend, Sienna acted instinctively. She caught the first with a heel kick to the head that sent him somersaulting backwards over the bench, clattering onto the concrete beyond. In her next movement, she hit the second man with a powerful blow to the solar plexus. He doubled up immediately and crumpled to the floor gasping for breath. The last of them was upon her before she had the chance to defend herself, but rather than resist his attack, she spun him around so she could get a proper strike in. But before she could reach him, Jutan had the man in a neck hold and, as she twisted hard, he gasped for air, pleading with her to stop.

'Ordinarily I wouldn't pick on someone who is weaker than me,' said Jutan, 'but you four seem to think that's perfectly acceptable.'

She looked at the man who had been brandishing the knife. He was sitting on the floor looking dazed and confused, nursing his jaw and his badly bruised ego.

'Now,' she said. 'Why don't you pick up that beer can and put it in the litter bin over there.'

They stared at one another for a few seconds but it was obvious who was going to blink first. He got to his feet, picked up the can and put it in the litter bin to the side of the bench.

When Jutan finally released the man from the neck grip, the four attackers just stood there as if they were waiting for permission to leave. Sienna was ready, in case they launched another attack, but Jutan seemed calm and composed.

'Right, on your way,' she said.

They turned and walked sullenly back towards the harbour, hoping desperately that no one had seen them being beaten up by an old lady and a girl. As they did, the man on the bench blinked several times as if he was coming out of a dream.

'Who are you people?' he said. 'I've never seen you two around here before.'

'No, we're from Weymouth,' said Jutan. 'We breed them much harder around our way. These Bramlington kids are lightweights.'

She dipped into her bag and gave the man some money, suggesting he get himself some lunch at the café, but having thanked them both for their help he promptly went back to sleep.

Despite the altercation they had just been in, Jutan was still impeccably dressed and totally unruffled, and while they made their way back along the promenade she carried on briefing Sienna as if nothing had happened.

'There's one other thing you should know,' she said. 'There are some rogue elements inside the British government that have been giving the security services cause for concern. In fact we think Osorio may have recruited a government minister to his cause. That mind control plot you discovered on Kestrel Island would have needed someone on the inside to administer the drugs, and our contacts think that all the evidence points to the Home Secretary Harry Jacobs.'

'But why would a member of the government side

with Osorio against his own people?' said Sienna.

'Power,' Jutan answered. 'Jacobs is an immensely ambitious man but he's also a liability. Fortunately, the United Kingdom has a strong Prime Minister who is capable of keeping him in his place. But if Osorio had gained an element of control over the British government, he could have built a substantial power base here, which would have assisted him greatly in his quest to take control on Galacdros. Your father and the other senators have worked tirelessly to protect our world from Osorio and his rebel forces, so it's vital we continue to disrupt his efforts here in this world.'

As they parted company, Jutan wished Sienna good luck in her mission and reminded her how proud her father was.

'And remember one other thing, Sienna,' said Jutan. 'Your mission is not to bring Osorio to justice. It is to locate The Orb and return it to its rightful place in the Senate. And this must be done with the minimum of fuss. You must not involve the British police or security services for any reason. The existence of Galacdros and the relationship between our two worlds is something very few people know about. It is vital you don't attract attention to your activities as it would be awkward to explain away your presence here.'

Sienna stood and watched Jutan as she walked off towards the coast road. Despite her advanced years, she was an immensely impressive figure. Strong, courageous and wise, she strode purposefully forward with an air of confidence and dignity. She may not have had youth on her side but she was a great advertisement for living an impeccable life.

CHAPTER 4

The overnight rain had cleared to the east, so Sophie decided she would walk into the town to meet Sienna at the train station. She had been up since seven o'clock, which was unusual for her during the school holidays, but she was so excited about seeing her friend again she had found it hard to sleep. Gripping a piece of toast between her teeth, she slipped on her jacket and scarf and bolted out of the house to head into town. Sienna's train was due to arrive at 10.34, but Sophie wanted to get to the station well before that. She would hate for Sienna to step off the train and not be able to see a friendly face.

When she reached the town centre, the open air market was bustling with energy as swarms of hungry shoppers feasted their eyes on the vast array of goods that were on sale. There were traders selling crockery, pot plants and mirrors and a host of food stands whose sweet and spicy smells wafted through the air, tempting the taste buds of anyone passing by. There was a wool and needlecraft stall, someone selling old vinyl records and a stall displaying hand-made jewellery that really caught Sophie's eye. She would have loved to stop and take a good look at it all but she knew there wasn't time. Sienna's train was due to arrive in less than fifteen minutes.

A trader with a handcart backed into her, knocking her off balance for a moment, but she just smiled and accepted his apology. It seemed like nothing could dampen her mood this morning. She was too excited about seeing Sienna to let anything bring her down.

But then her eyes were drawn to the other side of the square, and she saw a face she had only seen recently in her waking nightmares. She gasped and stood rooted to the spot, too stricken with fear to react. It was Osorio. He was quite a distance away, buying vegetables from one of the market traders, but there was no mistaking that face. The pale skin, the hair drawn severely back from the forehead and the dark goatee beard, it was definitely him.

She swallowed hard, and for a few moments she found it difficult to breathe, then Osorio turned his gaze in her direction and for a split second they were eye to eye. It sent an icy chill right through to her bones to be face to face with his evil stare again. It was like being hit by a bolt of lightning. She darted behind a pillar hoping he hadn't spotted her, but she knew that it was probably too late.

How could this be happening? In a second her world had been turned upside down. Images flashed into her mind of that night on Kestrel Island and the terror she felt as she and Sienna were shot at and hunted down like animals. The thought of it made her break into a cold sweat.

What could Osorio be doing in Hampton Spa? Of all the towns in the country why did he pick this one? She tentatively peered around from behind the pillar hoping to see someone who looked quite like Osorio but obviously wasn't him. Perhaps she had imagined it. Perhaps in her excitement about seeing Sienna again her mind had started to play tricks on her. There are plenty of men with dark goatee beards. Maybe it was a trick of the light.

Who was she kidding? It was definitely Osorio. The horror of her experience on Kestrel Island had burned the image of his face into her brain. She'd recognise him anywhere and now, for some reason, he had turned up in her home town.

She felt a desperate urge to run, to put as much distance between herself and Osorio as possible. For all she knew he may be dashing across the market right now. Perhaps there were others with him and they were fanning out through the market trying to get to her before she could get away.

As she rushed from the square, there wasn't a spring in her step any more. She felt vulnerable and isolated and was constantly looking over her shoulder to see who was walking behind her. Sitting alone in the station, waiting for the train to arrive, she was terrified that Osorio and his henchmen could appear at any moment and by the time Sienna arrived her fate would have been sealed. It was an agonising wait.

Finally the train trundled into the station, and as the passengers started to disembark Sophie spotted Sienna at the back of the line, her proud face framed by her short dark hair. Three months had passed since they'd last seen one another, but Sienna looked just as vibrant and powerful as she had the day the girls first met. It was a relief to see her looking so robust and healthy.

The girls had a big hug and there were lots of smiles

and fast talking about the journey, but Sienna quickly realised that all was not well. She paused and looked at Sophie with her dark, penetrating eyes.

'What's wrong?' she said.

Sophie hesitated for a moment. She was still trembling a little and didn't want to lose her composure, but Sienna had already guessed it involved Osorio. She was highly skilled at mind reading and she and Sophie had established a telepathic link during the time they spent together in Bramlington Bay.

'It's Osorio, isn't it?' said Sienna, her eyes widening with excitement.

'Erm…Yes,' Sophie answered. 'How did you know?'

'You're transmitting some very powerful images. Are you sure it was him though?'

'Well, I only saw him from the other side of the market but it was definitely Osorio. After everything we went through on Kestrel Island, that's not a face I'm going to forget in a hurry.'

'So he's already here then,' said Sienna.

'Already here?' said Sophie, shocked that Sienna didn't seem surprised at the news. 'Were you expecting him then?'

'In a way,' said Sienna. 'Just before I left Bramlington

Bay, I met up with one of our agents from Galacdros, and she thinks Osorio may be in Kent looking for a Galacdrian scientist called Professor Felso.'

'What, in Hampton Spa?' said Sophie, barely able to believe what she was hearing.

'Well, not necessarily Hampton Spa, but they think he could be somewhere in Kent.'

Sophie was totally flabbergasted. It was shocking enough to have spotted Osorio in the market but the idea that a scientist from Galacdros might be living in her home town just left her speechless.

'Did you get the chance to follow Osorio, to see where he went next?' said Sienna, picking up her large rucksack and slipping it onto her shoulder.

'No,' said Sophie. 'To be honest, I was so terrified when I saw him that I just wanted to get right away from there as quickly as possible. And I may have imagined this, but while I was looking at him he turned and, for a moment, I thought our eyes met.'

'So he may have seen you then?'

'Unfortunately, I think he did, which isn't good news is it?'

'It's not ideal,' said Sienna. 'If Osorio knows you're in Hampton Spa then it's reasonable for him to think that I'm here too, so we'd better be on our guard from now on. Can we store my rucksack somewhere? I'd like to go straight to the market just in case he's still there?'

'To the market?' said Sophie.

The truth was Sophie would rather have done anything than come face to face with Osorio again. It was one thing wanting to be as fit and powerful as Sienna, but she had no desire to get involved in another life or death struggle.

But Sienna was adamant. She'd come to this world to retrieve The Orb and to do that she would have to find Osorio and work out how to take it from him. If there was any chance he was still in the town, she wanted to follow him back to wherever he was staying then devise a plan of attack.

They stored Sienna's rucksack at the station then made their way quickly through the town to the market. At times the crowds were so thick it was difficult to move freely, but there was no sign of Osorio anywhere. After about half an hour they found a quiet spot in a doorway and stopped to gather their thoughts.

'No sign of him,' said Sienna, despondently. 'OK, perhaps we'd better start looking for Professor Felso then. What's the best way to search the local records to see if there's any mention of him?'

'We could look online,' said Sophie.

She pulled out her phone, tapped the Google app and thumbed in the name Professor Felso. They stood and waited for the results but nothing was coming up.

'Oh no, this is taking ages,' she said. 'It's always a problem trying to get a decent signal around here. Let's go back to the house and have a look on the laptop.'

'OK,' said Sienna. 'We can leave my rucksack at the station. I'll pick it up tomorrow.'

When they arrived at the house, Sophie turned on the laptop and typed Professor Felso into Google, but most of the search results were in a foreign language. Then they tried Felso/Hampton Spa which was much more revealing. They found an article from three years ago about someone called Felso being prosecuted for refusing to fill out the census form. It said he lived in a house called Heath Grange which turned out to be a large sprawling property on the outskirts of Crook's Wood.

'I think I know that house,' said Sophie. 'It's a big house that's set back from the road as you go out of town towards Sevenoaks. Whenever we pass it in the car I always imagine it belongs to an artist or a writer. It has such a romantic feel to it, so close to the wood, with the lake sprawling out behind it.'

'We should go there and take a look,' said Sienna.

Sophie looked a little alarmed.

'What now?' she said.

'Why wait?' Sienna answered. 'Now Osorio knows you're in Hampton Spa, the more we know about his circumstances the safer you'll be. Is it a long way to the house?'

'Well, it's at the other side of Crook's Wood,' said Sophie, 'so it would take quite a while to get there on foot.'

'And what else did you have planned for this afternoon?' Sienna asked, with an impish smile.

'Well, I thought I might hide under the bed for a few hours until word came through that Osorio had moved to Australia,' said Sophie.

Sienna chuckled and nudged her arm.

'What happened to that warrior queen you turned into on Kestrel Island?'

'It's her afternoon off,' Sophie answered.

They sat in silence for a few seconds. Sophie was reluctant to get involved in another battle with Osorio, but she knew Sienna would go out to Heath Grange anyway and would need someone to show her the way. Like it or not, she would have to tag along with her. After all, that's what friends are for.

'So, we're just going to take a look, are we?' she asked. 'We're not going to attack anyone and then be chased through the wood by armed guards?'

'No, I just want to take a look at the house.'

That was exactly the answer Sophie wanted to hear. They were just going to take a look. Although she knew Sienna wouldn't be able to resist launching an assault if the opportunity presented itself. This whole situation was starting to develop an unfortunate feeling of déjà vu.

CHAPTER 5

Sophie felt exhilarated to be out walking with Sienna again. The time they'd spent together in the summer had been a complete game changer for her, opening her eyes to her true potential and inspiring her to aim a lot higher. Despite having reservations about going to Heath Grange, it was good to be back in Sienna's company.

They headed out of town on the Sevenoaks road then skirted around the outside of Crook's Wood towards the old house. Looking across at the densely packed trees, Sophie thought about Daniel Fletcher's claims that a monstrous creature was on the loose in the wood, and she wondered whether there could possibly be any truth in it.

'By the way,' she said, 'there are reports that a strange creature has been spotted in this wood recently. It was on the front page of this week's local paper. They're calling it "The Monster of Crook's Wood."'

'Monster?' said Sienna. 'Why? What does it look like?'

'Well, according to eyewitness Daniel Fletcher, it's eight feet tall and covered in hair. But Daniel Fletcher goes to my school, and he's famous for pranks and attention seeking, so I'm not sure I believe any of it.'

The edge of the wood was densely populated with bushes and shrubs and they had to force their way past them to get inside, but once they were under the canopy of the trees it was much easier to move around. Up ahead they could see the outline of Heath Grange through the occasional gaps in the foliage. They picked their way quietly through the wood then stopped a short distance from the house, crouching down behind a clump of bushes to watch for any movement inside.

In its day the house must have been a truly magnificent sight. It was a sprawling early Victorian mansion on two floors that spread out comfortably over the grounds. The garden to the front would have been beautifully landscaped at one point and the ivy that covered most of the west side would have been trimmed and properly maintained. Now the garden looked ramshackle and overgrown and the house was in need of a coat of paint, but the path up to the front door had recently been cleared and two of the downstairs windows were open. These were the only signs that someone might be living there.

They watched and listened for several minutes looking for any further signs of life, but nothing and nobody stirred. Just as Sienna was wondering what to do, the front door opened and a young man in jeans and a white T shirt appeared carrying a broom. He brushed away diligently at the front step and pathway then went back inside and shut the door. The girls looked at one another in surprise.

'Do you think that was Professor Felso?' said Sophie.

'I doubt it,' Sienna answered. 'I think Professor Felso is about the same age as my father. I don't know who that could have been.'

She sat and thought for a moment, trying to decide what they should do now.

'Let's work our way over to the other side of the house,' she said. 'We can use the wood as cover.'

Despite the cool autumnal weather many of the trees still retained a full covering of leaves, and once they were back in the heart of the wood it seemed dark and mysteriously murky. It was as if they were walking in twilight. Sophie had known of this wood since she was a small child and used to love wandering through the trees with her dad whenever her family visited the picnic area, but now she was struck by how much of a wilderness it was.

This was the domain of the small animals and birds that had made the wood their home. Humans may dominate whatever happened on the outside of these trees but in here a different pecking order existed. She wondered how many small pairs of eyes were on them at that moment, waiting for them to pass so the wood could return to normality. It felt untamed and primeval, and Sophie found it slightly unnerving.

They'd only been walking for a minute or so when Sienna stopped suddenly and stood looking straight ahead. She seemed transfixed by something in the distance, and when Sophie saw what had captured her attention she gasped and stepped back in terror. It was the tall, sinister figure of Osorio. He was about fifty yards in front of them, walking slowly through the wood, and he appeared to be deep in thought.

Sophie wanted to run. She wanted to get as far away from this place as possible. She was still mentally scarred from the events on Kestrel Island and the last thing she wanted to do was get involved in another battle with Osorio. She glanced across at Sienna, hoping they were going to withdraw to devise a plan of action, but Sienna was already moving in Osorio's direction. Oblivious to what was going on around her, she was like a lion with the scent of a zebra in its nostrils and she seemed determined not to let her prey escape. With a heavy heart Sophie trailed along after her, feeling as if she was heading into another life or death situation.

But when they reached the spot where they'd seen Osorio, he was nowhere to be found. They searched the area thoroughly for several minutes, watching and listening for any sign of movement, but there was no trace of him anywhere. Sienna shook her head in bewilderment.

'Where is he?' she said.

'I don't know,' Sophie replied. 'Maybe he heard us coming and decided to …. What was that?'

They spun around and, for a brief moment, Sienna caught a glimpse of Osorio's head in some bushes at the other side of a clearing. He was moving quickly now, possibly aware that he was no longer alone in the wood, but by the time they'd managed to cross to where she'd seen him there was no sign of him there either. He seemed to have completely vanished.

'He's just disappeared into thin air,' said Sienna. 'This is impossible. Where is he?'

She sat down on the trunk of a fallen tree, shaking her head and feeling as if she'd been hoodwinked or outmanoeuvred.

'Maybe he's learned to become invisible,' said Sophie, trying to find an explanation.

'Invisible?' said Sienna, in a mocking tone. 'I think you've been reading too many of those fantasy adventure books you like.'

Sophie smiled.

'Well, OK,' she said, 'that suggestion was a bit absurd, but six months ago if someone had told me I was about to become friends with a girl from another world I'd have thought that was even more ridiculous.'

'Alright,' said Sienna, 'we'll keep the possibility that he's invisible open for the time being. I can't think how else he could have done it.'

She stood up and looked all around her. Much as she hated to admit it, there was no point in continuing their search.

'We ought to get back to the town,' she said. 'If Osorio really did spot us, he'll be a long way from here by now.'

Sophie didn't need to be asked twice. She'd been reluctant to go out to Heath Grange in the first place and now they had spotted Osorio she was more than happy to get out of the wood. Having scanned the surrounding area one more time, and still found no sign of Osorio, they turned and started making their way slowly back towards the town.

It was late afternoon and the light of the day had already started to fade, making the wood seem even darker and more sinister than before. Sophie thought about Daniel Fletcher's monster story, and every time she sensed movement in the shadows his claims started to sound a lot more plausible. She was beginning to feel a little spooked.

To make matters worse, Sienna appeared to be deep in thought and whenever Sophie tried to engage her in conversation she wasn't really concentrating on what was being said. It wasn't like her at all. She was normally so sharp and alert, totally tuned in to whatever was going on around her.

Then after they'd been walking for about five minutes Sienna casually leaned across and whispered in Sophie's ear.

'Don't turn around, but I think someone is following us.'

Sophie's eyes widened in alarm.

'I'm not sure who it is,' said Sienna, 'but I've been picking up their thoughts for the last few minutes.'

They walked a little further and, as they did, Sophie tried to sense the presence of whoever might be nearby, but without any luck. She heard a branch snap behind her to the left and immediately thought of Daniel Fletcher's story again. Could it possibly be true? Were they about to be attacked by a monstrous creature?

When they reached a clearing, Sienna spun around and for a split second she caught a glimpse of someone or something darting behind a tree. Motioning to Sophie to stay where she was, she slowly approached the tree ready to do battle.

'I know you're hiding behind that tree,' she said. 'You moved behind it much too late.'

She stood and waited for a reaction. Several seconds passed.

'I can see your shoe,' said Sienna.

After a wait of another few seconds, a figure slowly emerged from behind the tree. Sienna didn't recognise him but Sophie did immediately.

'Oh no, it's you,' she shouted. 'Why are you following us, and what are you doing in this wood anyway?'

'I might ask you the same question,' said the man, looking at the girls suspiciously.

'Who is this?' Sienna asked.

'His name is Will Starkey,' said Sophie, 'and he's a reporter for The Daily Press. He's supposed to be in town covering the visit of the Prime Minister but for some reason he's decided to follow us through the wood instead.'

'What makes you think I was following you?' said Starkey. 'This is a public place. I'm entitled to wander around just as much as you are.'

'You've been following us for about five minutes,' said Sienna sharply. 'Are you some sort of weirdo?'

Starkey visibly bristled.

'If you must know I'm here on business,' he said. 'I'm investigating the sightings of this so called "Monster of Crook's Wood" and I wouldn't be surprised to find out that you two have something to do with it.'

'What are you talking about?' said Sophie. 'How on earth could you think it was something to do with us?'

'Well, you kids would love to be able to hoax the newspapers wouldn't you? But I'm not that easily fooled.'

He held up his phone and waved it at them provocatively.

'And I've got a few photos here of you two acting suspiciously in this wood that I think will be a great addition to the story I'm working on. "Monster hoax exposed. Daughter of Green Party candidate caught out." It should help your mother disappear without trace in this week's election campaign.'

'Shall I take the phone away from him?' Sienna asked, looking at Sophie.

Starkey scoffed, but took a step back when he was met by Sienna's steely glare.

'No, he'll only get the police involved,' Sophie answered. 'Let's just leave him to it and get back to the town.'

'Yes, well just remember. I've got my eye on you two,' said Starkey, slipping the phone back into his pocket.

'And I've got my eye on you,' said Sienna, threateningly. 'So stop following us around. Go and find your monster, you'll probably find you have a lot in common.'

The girls turned and continued walking back towards the town, but Starkey was determined not to be shaken off.

'Where did you hide the monster costume?' he shouted after them. 'I'm going to find it eventually, so you might as well just tell me now.'

When they didn't respond he refused to give up.

'Give me the exclusive story, and I could turn you two into local celebrities.'

Once again the girls didn't respond. They didn't even turn around. They just kept walking back towards the town as Starkey's shouts became less and less audible.

'Are you sure that was Osorio we saw back there?' said Sophie, as they approached the edge of the wood. 'I mean, the light wasn't that good. You don't think it could have been Starkey do you?'

'No, it was definitely Osorio,' Sienna answered. 'He has such a distinctive appearance I'd recognise him anywhere.'

Sophie knew Sienna was right. Osorio was tall and slim, with dark hair and a dark goatee beard. Starkey looked nothing like that.

'And even if that had been Starkey,' Sienna continued, 'how did he just disappear like that? If anyone was going to be able to vanish into thin air it's much more likely to have been Osorio. No, there's something weird going on here, something we don't know all the facts about yet.'

It was almost dark when they arrived back at Sophie's house and, having spent the afternoon outside, it felt good to be inside in the warm. Sophie went straight back onto the laptop to do another search on Heath Grange and, after trawling around for a while, she found a website called History of Kent that included some interesting information on the house. It was once the headquarters of a notorious family of nineteenth century smugglers and when the authorities finally arrested the gang they discovered a labyrinth of tunnels under the house in which they stored their ill gotten gains. The tunnels were quite extensive and even had a secret exit into Crook's Wood in case the gang needed to make a hasty exit.

'So that's how Osorio managed to disappear,' said Sienna. 'He must have darted into the hidden entrance to the tunnels.'

'So I think we can assume that he's staying at Heath Grange,' said Sophie, 'and he's working with Professor Felso.'

The website also gave details of a book about the gang's story that contained a detailed map of the tunnels. It was called "Bandits and Smugglers of Kent" and, even though it had been out of print for many years, Sophie thought they might be able to find a copy in one of the antiquarian bookshops in the town.

'If that book is available anywhere in the county, it'll be in one of the bookshops in this town,' she said. 'I'll start phoning around first thing tomorrow morning.'

CHAPTER 6

'Avalon Books!' said Sophie, bursting into the kitchen, smiling broadly.

Sienna was sitting at the table, finishing off her breakfast. She looked a little confused.

'What about Avalon Books?' she said.

'They've got a copy of "Bandits and Smugglers of Kent" and they're holding it for me until lunchtime. I decided to phone the bookshops in alphabetical order and good old Avalon Books came up trumps.'

'Well, lucky the only copy wasn't in Zodiac Books,' said Sienna. 'We'd have been here all morning.'

'Good one,' said Sophie, smiling back at her. 'I told the man I'd pick it up at about ten o'clock.'

'That's great,' said Sienna. 'While you're there I can go back to the station and collect my rucksack.'

Sophie looked a little taken aback.

'Are you sure that's a good idea?' she said. 'Now Osorio knows we're here, shouldn't we stick together when we're in the town?'

'Well, it won't be for long,' said Sienna. 'Provided we keep our wits about us we should be OK. Let's face it, the sooner we can get started the better.'

Sophie reluctantly agreed, although she still wasn't sure what they were going to get started on.

'OK,' she said. 'I suppose it should be alright. There's a lovely little cafe on Market Square. Perhaps we could meet there once we've picked up our stuff. We can have tea and cake and study the book.'

'Excellent,' said Sienna. 'And keep your eyes open as you move around the town. If you catch sight of Osorio anywhere text me, and I'll get over there as soon as I can.'

Entering Avalon Books was like stepping back in time. There was a slightly musty smell about the shop even though it was impeccably maintained, and everywhere Sophie looked there were old books stacked up to the ceiling. Hardbacks, paperbacks, leather bound volumes that were as old as the building, their corners faded from years of being handled. There were countless vintage book collections, many of which would have been rescued from an old attic or picked up at a car boot sale. Every available corner and surface was fully occupied.

The owner of the shop was an elderly book enthusiast who dressed like someone from another century. He wore a three piece suit with a spotted bow tie and his pocket watch had a gold chain that stretched across his waistcoat, matching his elegant gold cufflinks.

'Good morning,' said Sophie, smiling politely. 'I reserved a book this morning. "Bandits and Smugglers of Kent."'

'Oh yes,' said the man. 'I remember.'

He took a stack of small cards out of a drawer and flipped through them at incredible speed.

'Miss Watson isn't it?' he said, stopping about two thirds of the way through.

'Yes, that's right,' Sophie answered.

'If you wouldn't mind waiting a moment, I'll just get it for you.'

He pushed a large ladder on wheels out into the middle of the floor and positioned it against one of the sets of shelves. The book turned out to be right at the top and even though the shop layout seemed quite chaotic he knew exactly where it was.

'Here we are,' he said, perched at the top of the ladder, casually flipping through the book. Despite being precariously balanced, he was perfectly at home at the top of his ladder. He'd obviously been perching up there for most of his adult life.

It turned out to be quite a small book and it fitted perfectly in the inside pocket of Sophie's jacket. She thanked the man for holding it for her and, having paid him, made her way out of the shop and headed back to meet Sienna at the cafe.

When she reached the square, the market was in full swing and appeared to be even more crowded than usual. She looked at her watch. It was around this time yesterday that she'd spotted Osorio. Was it possible he could turn up at exactly the same time again today? The thought of it made her body tense up in panic. She ducked behind a pillar, making sure there was a good view of the stall she'd seen him at, but after a few minutes of keeping watch there was no sign of him anywhere. Yet she still couldn't shake off an overwhelming feeling of dread.

Suddenly, someone yelled her name at the far side of the market, and when she spun around she saw Sienna rushing across the square in her direction.

'Sophie, thank goodness I've found you,' she said, breathlessly. 'Quick, follow me, no time to explain.'

Without saying another word she sprinted from the square leaving Sophie wondering what was going on. This wasn't like Sienna at all. She was normally so calm and measured. What had happened to make her act with such urgency?

There was no alternative but to chase after her although that was easier said than done. Despite all the training Sophie had been doing since she'd returned to Hampton Spa she was no match for Sienna, and soon she was trailing quite a long way behind her.

'Hold on Sienna!' she shouted. 'Wait for me!'

When she turned the corner into Guildhall Street, Sienna was waiting a little further down the road, but once Sophie was within about twenty feet of her, she took off once more.

'It's not much further,' Sienna shouted, turning into a scruffy little side road.

Stopping at the top of some steps that led down to a basement, Sienna waited for a few seconds until she was sure Sophie had spotted her then she ran down the steps and in through the door at the bottom. By the time Sophie arrived she could barely breathe for the exertion she'd just made. She leaned against the wall, desperately trying to catch her breath, and looked down the steps towards the basement. The door had been left slightly open and the room was in total darkness.

'It's down here, Sophie,' she heard Sienna shout. 'It will all make sense once you're inside.'

Reluctantly, Sophie started making her way down the stairs. This was all too weird and not at all like Sienna. What was going on? Why hadn't she taken a few seconds to explain before rushing off? She paused at the door, unsure whether to continue. It was pitch black inside and she couldn't find a light switch anywhere.

'Come inside,' she heard Sienna shout. 'I'll explain everything in a minute.'

As soon as Sophie had taken a couple of steps into the basement, the door slammed shut behind her and someone flicked a switch, flooding the room with light.

As she looked around, the sight she was greeted with sent her mind into total confusion. Osorio was standing in front of the door, looking both menacing and triumphant, and Sienna was standing by the opposite wall next to two identical young men wearing T shirts and jeans. All three were smiling blandly at her.

'How nice of you to join us,' said Osorio.

The shock of seeing Osorio was so overwhelming that Sophie was unable to think straight. None of this made any sense. She just stood there, ashen faced, looking from Sienna to Osorio and back again.

'Sienna,' she said, still trying to catch her breath. 'What's going on?'

Sienna didn't respond. She just leaned back against the wall and carried on smiling blandly at her. Osorio could see the look of fear and panic on Sophie's face.

'I'm afraid she won't be able to answer you,' he said, enjoying Sophie's discomfort. 'It's not part of her programme.'

'Programme?' said Sophie. 'Sienna, what's he talking about?'

'I'm talking about artificial intelligence,' Osorio answered. 'When I first saw her, I thought she was a stunning likeness but I couldn't be sure she would fool anyone close to her. But now you have confirmed my initial thoughts. She is truly remarkable, and I am sure she will be perfect for the task I have planned for her.'

'Artificial intelligence?' said Sophie, looking at Sienna in confusion.

And then it finally sank in. This wasn't Sienna at all. It was an android built in her likeness. The chase through the streets had all been designed to lure Sophie into a trap and she hadn't suspected a thing. She felt as if she had been caught up in the web of a particularly venomous spider.

'If you look closely you'll notice they all have the same smile,' said Osorio, pointing at Sienna and the two young men. 'That's one of the small details Professor Felso still has to work out, but it would be picky of me to make an issue of it.'

He glared at Sophie with a triumphant look on his face.

'Your interference on Kestrel Island set my plans back considerably, but you should have learned to concentrate on your own affairs, my dear. Now you will pay the price for getting in out of your depth.'

He turned to the androids that were standing by the wall.

'Take her out to the house and lock her in one of the downstairs rooms,' he said. 'Tell Professor Felso I have some business to attend to in the town and I will be back shortly, and if the girl even thinks of trying to escape, kill her.'

CHAPTER 7

When Osorio left the basement, Sophie ran at the door in a desperate attempt to escape, but one of the android guards grabbed her by the arm and dragged her back into the room. He had a bland smile on his face but the words he spoke were menacing.

'I would advise you not to cause us any difficulties,' he said. 'If we are unable to carry out our orders we may have to destroy you.'

She tried to shake herself free but the android had a grip of iron on her arm.

'Now, we're going to walk up the steps and get into the car that's parked across the road,' he continued. 'If you give us any trouble, it'll be the last thing you do.'

They marched her up the steps and across the road to an old white car that was parked a little further down. Sophie was bundled into the back seat and, once they were all on board, the driver donned a baseball cap and a pair of dark glasses and pulled the car out into traffic. As they headed out of town towards the countryside, they looked like any other group of young people having a fun day out together. They all seemed so happy and smiley. Sophie didn't have to guess where they were heading. She was sure the house Osorio spoke of was Heath Grange and the downstairs rooms were part of the extensive labyrinth of tunnels.

On arriving at Heath Grange, the driver dragged Sophie from the back of the car and shoved her into the house through the kitchen door. He leaned against one side of a large bookcase that covered part of the far wall and it pivoted on a central axis, revealing a space behind and a staircase that led down into the darkness. They took Sophie by the arms and marched her down the steps. Nothing was said and Sophie knew there was no point in protesting. These were not people they were machines, high-tech machines that were operated by very sophisticated computers. It was all quite chilling.

At the bottom of the steps Sophie could tell they were now quite a way below ground level, in what appeared to be a large storage area with several tunnels leading off it. The guard wearing the baseball cap dragged her into one of the tunnels while the other two followed on behind them.

The tunnel was dimly lit and had been roughly hewn out of the earth, but it was large enough for everyone to stand up quite comfortably. It smelled musty and dank and the temperature had dropped by a couple of degrees. Everything seemed to be a shade of grey as if the colour had been sucked out of the world. Sophie wanted to scream out for help but she knew that it was pointless. The chances of anyone hearing her were close to zero.

After twisting and turning a few times they finally arrived at an enormous, well lit room that was kitted out like a laboratory. There were several large workbenches pushed up against the wall and on one of them a selection of synthetic body parts and some computer circuitry were scattered. A middle aged man was working at a desk over by the far wall. He was quite a small man, not much bigger than Sophie, and when they entered the room he stopped what he was doing and looked up. He seemed surprised and uncomfortable to see Sophie standing there.

'What's she doing here?' he said.

'Osorio told us to take her here,' said the guard with the baseball cap. 'She is to be locked in one of the small rooms at the end of the laboratory.'

'But she's just a girl,' said the man.

'Osorio told us she is to be locked in one of the rooms,' said the guard.

'Yes, I heard you,' said the man.

He stared at the android with a mixture of surprise and concern.

'Why are you wearing a baseball cap?' he asked.

The guard looked at him without answering.

'My name is Garth,' he said, eventually. 'Call me Garth.'

At this, the man looked a little alarmed.

'But you're an android,' said the man. 'Who gave you this name?'

'My name is Garth,' said the guard.

The man looked at him suspiciously then he turned towards Sophie.

'Who are you?' he said, 'and why are you here?'

Sophie swallowed hard. She could feel herself trembling, and she was desperately trying to keep control of her emotions.

'My name is Sophie Watson,' she said. 'And I don't know why.....'

'Professor Felso,' said the guard, interrupting Sophie

before she could answer fully. 'Osorio said…'

'Yes, yes, I know,' said Felso. 'Osorio told you to do something and you have to carry out his orders.'

He looked at Sophie and shook his head with the air of a man who had given up, then turned and went back to working at his desk.

The guard took some keys off a hook on the wall and marched Sophie down to the end of the laboratory. Eventually they reached a spot where the rudimentary shape of a door had been carved out of the earth. He pulled open the heavy wooden door and pushed Sophie inside.

For a brief moment, while the door was open, she was able to see inside the space. It was about the size of a small garden shed and felt even colder than it did in the tunnels. The guard didn't say anything before closing the door and locking it, and suddenly Sophie was alone and in total darkness. It was cold and damp and for a few seconds she just stood there staring into the blackness, gripped with terror and unable to think of what to do.

She took out her phone and flipped on the light. The tiny room was just a hole in the wall propped up by thick wooden posts that looked like they had been in place for many years. It was airless and there was a strong smell of earth. The chances of getting a phone signal this far under the ground were slim, but she tried to ring Sienna anyway, without any luck. The same thing happened when she tried to send a text.

What was she to do now? Before too long Osorio would return and he seemed determined to wreak revenge on the girls for disrupting his plans on Kestrel Island. She couldn't just stand in this hole in the ground and await her fate. She had to do something.

Perhaps she should have a go at telepathy. Sophie had never been convinced she could actually send or receive thoughts, but Sienna was insistent she had a natural ability and would become highly skilled if she practiced. She certainly seemed to have a strong connection with Sienna, and she was currently in such a heightened emotional state that it might just work.

Taking a few deep breaths to calm herself down, she closed her eyes and fixed her attention on Sienna, picturing in her mind a darkened room and images of Osorio and Heath Grange. Despite the doubts she had about her ability, she was desperate for this to work. Osorio could be on his way back to Heath Grange at that very moment, and what he may have in store for her was too horrible to contemplate. The thought of it made her focus her mind with even greater intensity. She had to make this work. It was her only hope.

CHAPTER 8

When Sienna reached the café, she was surprised to find that Sophie hadn't arrived yet. She considered walking around for a while to give Sophie a little more time to get there, but the table by the window was free so she decided it would make more sense to wait inside.

The cafe had a homespun charm and a comfortable easy feeling about it. It was light and spacious and the staff were warm and welcoming. There was a large map of the town on the wall and beside it a notice board that was covered with a host of small posters and business cards from people advertising their services. Dog walkers and cleaners, piano tutors and yoga teachers. They were all plastered onto the green baize board in the hope of picking up a bit of extra business.

Sienna bought a cup of tea, then took it over to the table at the window and sat down to wait. It was the middle of the morning and outside in the square workers were buzzing past, rushing to get to their next urgent appointment. It seemed to Sienna that almost everyone was either talking on their phone or tapping something into it. Nobody seemed to be engaged with life around them.

A lot of the people in the cafe seemed to know one another, or perhaps they just came in here every day to get away from the daily grind. The door opened and a large smiley man came in, whistling chirpily.

'Oh no, here comes trouble,' said the jovial woman behind the counter. 'What's it to be Arthur, the usual?'

Ten minutes passed and there was still no sign of Sophie. After twenty minutes Sienna was concerned that something might have happened. She took out her phone and thumbed in a text. When she didn't receive a reply she tried to phone but was diverted to voicemail. Then she started to pick up a vibration of thought and a feeling of fear and desperation.

Sienna could tell immediately that it was Sophie, and when she closed her eyes the images she picked up kept coming back to the same three things. Osorio's face, the view of Heath Grange from Crook's Wood, and the experience of being somewhere dark and enclosed. It didn't take a genius to work out what Sophie was trying to tell her. She must be in one of the tunnels under Heath Grange and in some way this involved Osorio. There was nothing else for it. She would have to go out to Heath Grange immediately and try to get Sophie out of there.

The map on the wall covered quite a large area and, after studying it for a couple of minutes, the route out to Heath Grange looked fairly straightforward. First she would have to go back to the station to drop off her luggage, then it was a right turn into Church Street and straight out of town on the Sevenoaks road.

Before leaving, she rummaged through one of the side pockets of her rucksack and fished out a couple of things that might come in useful. A miniature flashlight she'd bought in a scuba diving shop in Bramlington Bay and the knife with a carved handle her father had given her when she graduated from The Academy. The knife was wrapped up in its shoulder holster. She slipped it into the inside pocket of her jacket and turned on the flashlight to check the batteries. It threw out quite a strong beam for something so small.

On the journey out to Crook's Wood, intermittent thoughts from Sophie kept flashing into her mind, most of them filled with a powerful sense of dread and hopelessness. The intensity of the thoughts made her quicken her pace and when Heath Grange was visible in the distance, she left the road and slipped into the wood, creeping stealthily towards the trees that overlooked the house. There was no sign of anyone or anything. She took the knife and holster out of her pocket, slipped her jacket off and fitted the holster around her shoulders. When she put her jacket back on again the knife and holster weren't visible at all.

Flexing the fingers of her left hand, she clenched and unclenched her fist a few times to loosen up the muscles in her lower arm. Those long weeks her arm had been in a sling had allowed the muscles to lose their strength and tone, and at a time like this the last thing she needed was for her arm to stiffen up.

As she crouched behind a large oak tree, scrutinising the house and its surroundings, she couldn't possibly have known just how close the girls were to one another. In the labyrinth of tunnels that stretched out from under the house, Sophie was locked securely in one of the rooms that had been carved out of the earth, whilst twenty feet above her Sienna was watching the house, waiting for the right moment to launch her rescue attempt.

It was very quiet. She watched and waited for a few minutes but nothing changed. Then she looked more closely and noticed that the front door was slightly open. Not by a great deal, just slightly ajar. A more cautious person would have thought twice about walking in through the front entrance but Sienna was not that person. There was no point in just sitting and waiting. That front door was a call to action.

On reaching the gate, she could feel her stomach starting to tighten up. She tried not to worry about the pangs of fear that were percolating inside her. She'd practiced for this moment again and again. Her training instructors had always told her that fear was a natural part of combat, just notice it and accept it as part of the journey, but it wasn't a feeling she'd ever gotten used to.

Walking quickly up the path, making as little noise as possible, she eased the door open and peered inside. Beyond it was a long hallway with doors leading off on either side and she could see part of a kitchen through the open door at the far end. She stepped tentatively inside and crept towards the room on her right. As she did, she heard the front door close behind her, and when she turned around a young man was standing there smiling at her. It was the same young man she'd seen sweeping the front step the day before, only now he was wearing a baseball cap.

'Oh hello,' she said, 'I'm a bit lost. I was hoping someone could tell me how to get to Hampton Spa.'

The young man just looked at her and smiled strangely. Sienna found it a little unnerving.

'No? Oh well,' she said casually, 'perhaps I'll just go back out to the road and ask someone there.'

She moved towards the door but he stepped in front of her, still not saying anything.

'Come to join your little friend have you?' said a voice from behind her, a voice that sent fear coursing through her body.

When she spun around Osorio was standing at the kitchen door, staring impassively at her. Sienna knew she was in big trouble and would need to take decisive action. She dodged to the side and aimed a kick at the young man, catching him on the side of the head, but it didn't seem to have any effect on him at all. She caught him with a perfectly aimed blow to the solar plexus, that ought to have left him gasping for breath, but he just continued looking at her with that same eerie smile.

She had no idea that she was dealing with a machine. It threw her into total confusion. When she tried to throw another punch, the android caught her arm and spun her around, pinning both arms behind her back. As she struggled unsuccessfully to wriggle free, Osorio came to within a few steps of her and fixed her with his cold, black eyes. It was like being face to face with a shark.

'Didn't they teach you anything at that training school you attended?' he said. 'You walked into a trap and the most basic of traps at that. The Elite must really be scraping the barrel to have to recruit the likes of you.'

Up close, Sienna was struck by how much Osorio's face had aged. He was quite a few years younger than her father but he looked so much older. The years of bitterness were taking their toll, and his face was badly lined with the pain and anger of defeat.

'Take her downstairs and put her with the other one,' he said. Then he turned and smiled menacingly at Sienna.

'Once you've settled in my dear we can have a little chat. I'm sure you'll find it fascinating.'

CHAPTER 9

The android guard forced Sienna down to the end of the hallway then dragged her through the kitchen door and down the stairs into one of the dimly lit tunnels. She fought against him every step of the way but couldn't free herself from his vice-like grip.

As they entered the laboratory, the noise of their struggle made Professor Felso look up from his desk. He was alarmed by the rough treatment Sienna was receiving but before he could intervene the guard had marched her down to the other end of the laboratory, opened the door cut roughly into the wall and shoved her inside. She fell to the floor and lay there in the darkness for a few seconds until the light from Sophie's phone illuminated the room.

'Sienna, are you alright?' said Sophie, shocked at her friend's sudden arrival.

'Yes, I'm OK,' said Sienna, dragging herself to her feet, despondently.

'How did you find me?' Sophie asked. 'I tried to send you a telepathic message but I wasn't sure it would work.'

'Oh, it worked alright,' said Sienna, 'but unfortunately that's the only thing that has worked. For a start, that man who pushed me in here doesn't seem to feel any pain.'

'It's an android,' said Sophie. 'And there are more of them.'

Before she could continue, the door opened and two of the android guards dragged the girls out, marched them back to the top of the laboratory and forced them down into two battered old office chairs. Osorio stood over them with a satisfied smile on his face. He was clearly enjoying his moment of victory.

At the other side of the room, Professor Felso was tinkering with some electrical parts that were spread out across his desk. He was trying to focus on his work but he couldn't ignore the growing sense of discomfort he felt about the treatment the girls were receiving.

'Search them,' said Osorio.

The guards went through the girls' pockets and emptied the contents out onto a small table. When they found the phones they crushed them with their bare hands until they were an unrecognisable tangle of plastic. Sophie looked at the little book she had been carrying in her pocket, hoping desperately they wouldn't realise what it was, but the guard with the baseball cap was more interested in the knife he found when he searched the inside of Sienna's jacket. He pulled it out and ran his finger along the sharp edge before holding the blade against Sienna's throat and smiling the creepy smile.

'Put that away,' Osorio barked.

The guard hesitated for a moment, as if a rebellious thought might have occurred to him, then he stuffed the knife into his belt and took a step back. Osorio stared at him intently for a few seconds, determined to assert his authority, but when the guard took another step back Osorio turned his gaze upon the girls.

'So,' he said, 'we meet again. Only this time I intend to make sure it's the last time you are able to interfere in my affairs.'

Sienna stared back at him determined not to show any fear but Sophie wasn't feeling quite as defiant.

'Let her go,' said Sienna, indicating her head towards Sophie. 'She's not part of our quarrel. This is between you and The Elite.'

'If only I could,' said Osorio, trying to sound reasonable. 'Unfortunately you two meddled in my affairs just a bit too much on Kestrel Island, and now I'm going to have to get rid of both of you once and for all.'

On hearing this Professor Felso stopped what he was doing and stared at Osorio in shock. 'Get rid of both of you?' What was Osorio talking about? These two weren't dangerous spies or master criminals, they were young girls, and the brutal way they were being treated wasn't what Felso had signed up for.

Osorio took a step closer to Sienna. He was enjoying pressing home his advantage.

'The strange thing is,' he said, 'I've been looking for you lately. I wanted to thank you for carrying out your patriotic duty and ridding our world of the weak and complacent man who has stood in my way for too long. I speak, of course, of your father Memphis.'

'I'd never do anything to help you in your plans and you know it,' Sienna spat back at him.

'Well, maybe you wouldn't,' said Osorio, 'but I think I know someone who would. Sienna, would you come in here please.'

A door at the side of the laboratory opened and the

android Sienna walked into the room. Sienna gasped and looked at her in shock. The likeness was chilling. It was like looking in a mirror.

'Sienna,' said Osorio. 'Please tell these people what you have planned for the next few days.'

'Of course,' said the android. 'Tomorrow morning I will be going back to Galacdros for an urgent meeting with my father and as soon as we are alone together I will draw this gun and kill him.'

She drew a gun from inside her jacket. It was a small handgun which Sienna knew would be fairly easy to conceal.

'Thank you, Sienna,' said Osorio.

The android smiled her strange smile then stood by the wall, staring into space.

Sienna felt totally wrong-footed by this development. She was the one person who could get close to her father without needing special security clearance, and by the time Memphis realised something was wrong it might be too late. The android was even wearing the same clothes as her, but that wouldn't have been difficult for Osorio to guess. Sienna always wore the same style of clothing and was as predictable as Jutan said she was. In fact, if she hadn't been wearing her red bandana she would have been indistinguishable from this android.

'The glorious thing about this plan,' said Osorio, 'is that once she has carried out her task, my associates on Galacdros will dispose of her discreetly and history will show that Memphis was murdered by his only daughter. What a fitting end to a pathetic life.'

Sienna was experiencing a massive inner turmoil but she was determined not to let it show.

'Of course, I couldn't have accomplished any of this until I had taken you out of circulation,' Osorio continued, 'so it was very considerate of you to walk in here today and save me the trouble of having to search for you.'

Professor Felso had been watching all this from the other side of the room, looking more and more uncomfortable. He was unsettled by the presence of the girls in the tunnels and now he knew that one of them was the daughter of Memphis, he realised he couldn't stay silent. He strode over to where Osorio was standing and grabbed hold of his arm.

'You didn't tell me that android was designed to mimic the daughter of Memphis,' he said, forcefully, 'or that you were planning to carry out an assassination.'

'You don't need to know every last detail of the plan

Felso,' Osorio replied. 'Please leave the politics to me.'

'This isn't politics!' Felso shouted. 'This is murder.'

Osorio rounded on him and grabbed him by his shirt.

'I don't intend to discuss anything else with you,' he said. 'You promised me there would be at least thirty of these guards by now and so far all you've managed is eight. Now get on with your work or I may have to ask one of the guards you so painstakingly built to teach you to take a more civil tone with me.'

He pushed Felso roughly back against some shelves, knocking several files to the floor in the process. As he did, the guard with the baseball cap took a couple of steps forward.

'Would you like me to hurt him?' he said.

'No, that won't be necessary,' Osorio answered, looking a little surprised at the guard's question.

'My name is Garth,' said the guard.

Osorio looked at him quizzically then glanced over at Professor Felso. They both realised that all was not as it should be with this android.

'So, Felso,' said Osorio, 'it seems you're not the master craftsman that you claim to be. Late with your deliveries and now the goods are starting to malfunction.'

'Maybe I should hurt him,' said the guard.

Osorio turned and looked at him.

'Take your place behind that chair,' he commanded.

The guard hesitated for a few seconds then walked back and stood behind Sienna's chair.

Professor Felso was clearly rattled by Osorio's reaction and seemed reluctant to take his protest any further. When he was a younger man he would have acted without considering the consequences, thrown his lot in with the girls because it was the right thing to do. But over the years he had become more cautious and pragmatic, learning to keep his thoughts and feelings to himself. He wasn't sure if he liked this new version of himself all that much. It was a wretched feeling and it gnawed away at his insides. He straightened up his shirt and walked slowly back to his workbench. As he did, Osorio turned to face the girls.

'If only he could make an android of himself,' he said. 'It would make life so much easier,'

'And that's the only way you'll ever be able to command loyalty,' said Sienna. 'Real people will never follow you because your threats will only work for so long.'

'The people will follow me because they know that I

have this,' he said, putting his hand into the pocket of his jacket and pulling out a small stone. It was smooth and shiny, about the size of a golf ball. He laid it on the palm of his hand and displayed it to the girls.

'When the people of Galacdros know that I possess The Orb it will inspire them to give me their loyalty,' he said. 'Of all the myths and legends our pathetic leaders push at us, the legend of The Orb is the only one the people believe with any real passion. And all the time it is in my possession I will continue to grow stronger.'

He brazenly displayed The Orb to Sienna, taunting her for his own amusement.

'When you briefly took The Orb from me on Kestrel Island you may have imagined that the battle was won,' he continued, 'but during these last three months I have grown stronger and more powerful and when I return triumphantly to Galacdros the people will recognise me as their true leader.'

He was so preoccupied with basking in the glory of his imagined victory that he didn't notice Professor Felso moving across the laboratory towards him. In a moment of liberation and wild impetuosity, Felso rushed across the room, grabbed The Orb off Osorio's hand and ducked out through the door into the tunnels.

It all happened so quickly that nobody moved for a few seconds then the shock of what had happened woke Osorio from his reverie.

'Get after him,' he screamed at the guards. 'Drag him back here, even if you have to break every bone in his body.'

CHAPTER 10

The guards and android Sienna bolted towards the door, fanning out into the tunnels to hunt for Professor Felso. Osorio was seething. He took a small handgun out of his jacket and paced back and forward, consumed with frustration and anger.

'Don't get your hopes up,' he said, looking contemptuously across at the girls. 'He built those androids for speed and agility. He'll be a victim of his own genius.'

Despite the perilous situation the girls were in, Sophie's mood had been lifted by Professor Felso's audacious action. It was heartening to know that they weren't alone in this underground prison and there was still a chance they could make it out alive.

But she wasn't expecting Professor Felso to be caught so quickly. Outside in the tunnels there was a commotion of shouting, and seconds later the guard wearing a baseball cap dragged Felso back into the laboratory, pushed him down into a chair and held him there with one hand. It looked as if there had been a bit of a struggle and Felso had definitely come off worse. There was a trace of blood under his nose and one of the pockets of his lab coat was ripped and torn. The guard handed something to Osorio who took it from him and put it into his jacket pocket.

'I was a fool to trust you, Felso,' said Osorio. 'You have a tremendous gift for creating these androids but you are dim witted on all other matters. Fortunately, I took the precaution of having an alternative plan should you fail me, and I will now have to put this into practice.'

'Shall I hurt him?' said Garth, the android with the baseball cap. 'He has been disloyal to you. I should hurt him.'

Osorio narrowed his eyes and looked at Professor Felso menacingly.

'No, that won't be necessary,' he said. 'The Professor is about to die.'

There was a wide-eyed and crazed look on his face, as if he was enjoying the power he had over his captives. He raised the small hand gun he was holding and pointed it directly at Felso's head.

'I had hoped that you would deliver more guards to me before I had to dispense with your services,' he said, 'but this treachery will be your last act.'

Sophie was frozen with fear. She couldn't believe she was about to witness the taking of another life. It was cold-blooded murder but all she could do was look on in horror, praying for some sort of miracle to occur.

What happened next was so staggering and unexpected that it took everyone completely by surprise. A monstrous and inhuman creature burst through the door of the laboratory and let out a terrifying howl of anger. Its massive apelike frame towered over everyone else in the room and its face was the stuff of nightmares, with demonic red eyes and two rows of sharp yellowing teeth. The creature was clearly in a rage and looked powerful enough to destroy anything in its path. Sophie gasped and grabbed hold of Sienna's arm in a panic.

As the creature took a step forward, Osorio turned and fired the gun repeatedly but the bullets appeared to have no effect on it at all. Instead it lumbered towards Osorio and smashed its massive arm against his chest, knocking him across the room into the wall at the far side of the laboratory. The guards all rushed towards the creature, desperate to protect Osorio from further attacks, and in the struggle that followed Professor Felso saw the chance for them to make their escape.

'Let's go,' he said, leaping to his feet.

The girls didn't need to be asked twice. They grabbed their belongings off the table and fled from the room, following Professor Felso through the twisting, turning tunnels he knew so well. They were determined to get as far away from Osorio as possible.

Back in the laboratory, the creature was running amok. Despite being up against four of Osorio's guards it was more than holding its own, and it was taking all of the androids' strength to keep it away from Osorio. The floor was littered with papers, fragments of glass and bits of broken furniture from the momentous battle that was taking place. It looked like there had been an explosion.

Osorio struggled to his feet trying to ignore the searing pain that was burning in his chest. He was dazed and winded but his intense anger was still driving him forward.

'Get it into that room over there,' he shouted, pointing at a storage section to the side of the laboratory.

The guards all jumped at the creature and managed to pin its massive hairy frame against the wall. It was a desperate struggle. As they shuffled and dragged it towards the small storeroom, the creature roared and howled in anger. It wasn't going in there without a fight. In the intensity of the battle there was a moment when it almost broke free, but eventually they managed to push it through the door and, as it stumbled and fell to the ground, they hurriedly turned the key and locked it securely inside.

'Get some of this furniture up against the door,' Osorio shouted. 'It might slow the thing down for a while.'

While the guards piled furniture up against the door, Osorio made radio contact with the androids that were out in the tunnels and ordered them to be on the lookout for Felso and the girls.

'If you see any of them, kill them on sight,' he barked. 'None of them are to get out of here alive.'

Inside the storeroom the creature was going berserk. It was clearly in a rage, and when its mighty fist punched a hole in the door Osorio realised it was time to leave. He turned to address the assembled guards.

'OK,' he said. 'Split up and comb these tunnels, and

if you find Felso or either of those girls make sure they're dead before you leave them.'

Further down the tunnels the girls and Professor Felso paused for a moment to decide on a plan of action. Felso was leaning against the wall, breathing hard. It had been a long time since he'd had to exert himself to this extent, and it was taking him a while to catch his breath.

'They'll expect us to go straight for the exit into Crook's Wood,' he said, 'so we'll have to avoid that area for the time being. The androids are quicker and more powerful than us but they can't really think for themselves. They'll look for us in the most obvious places to start with.'

He took a couple of deep breaths in an effort to calm himself.

'What happened back there?' said Sophie. 'What was that monster that attacked Osorio?'

Felso looked at her and smiled.

'Oh, that wasn't a monster,' he said. 'That was the project I was working on before Osorio appeared on my doorstep. I call it Titan.'

'Titan?' said Sophie.

'Yes,' said Felso. 'It means someone who is god-like,

powerful and influential. Osorio hates it, so it was very satisfying to see him get clattered like that.'

'So it's another android,' said Sienna.

'Yes,' Felso answered. 'For years I've been trying to build androids with rudimentary human characteristics and that creature is my current prototype. Over the months I've developed quite a soft spot for it and I'm pleased to say it's very loyal to me.'

'But why did you make it look so terrifying?' Sophie asked.

Felso smiled and shook his head.

'Well, it seems stupid now,' he said, 'but I was bored with making the same humanoid forms for my experiments, and I wanted to explore something more interesting and exciting. I suppose I thought I was like Dr Frankenstein. Unfortunately, Titan has been malfunctioning a lot lately and wandering off into Crook's Wood.'

'So that would explain the sightings of a monster in the wood,' said Sophie.

'Monster in the wood?' said Felso, looking a little alarmed.

'Yes, it's been all over the local paper. It scared off some teenagers last week but most people think it's just a hoax.'

'I was worried something like that might happen,' said Felso, 'but I thought I'd been getting away with it. There's something wrong with its circuitry, I can't quite work out what it is. And that may not be the only problem. Something strange seems to be happening with one of the guards.'

'Do you mean the one that calls itself Garth?' Sophie asked.

'Yes,' said Felso. 'The guards were programmed to be totally obedient to Osorio and to operate without any emotions, but that one has been acting very strangely. Be careful if you encounter it down here. I think it's becoming quite unstable.'

'But how do you stop these androids?' said Sienna, 'they seem to be indestructible.'

'Their only vulnerable area is their knees but it would need quite a force to incapacitate them. Unfortunately, most of the important circuitry is inside their head, which is encased in a bulletproof material. To do any real damage you'd need to get a bullet in through their mouth and then up into their skull.'

He stopped for a moment, thinking he'd heard something, but when they listened intently all they could hear was the silence.

'The androids are programmed to move at great speed,' Felso continued, 'but they're not very quiet, so at least we'll have advanced warning of any attack.'

'What made you grab The Orb back there?' Sienna asked. 'That was the last thing I was expecting to happen.'

'Well, I had to do something,' said Felso. 'Now that I know more about Osorio's murderous plans I couldn't just stand by and let it happen. To be honest, it was the act of a desperate man.'

'Well, it was very brave of you,' said Sophie.

'Brave or foolhardy,' said Felso, smiling at her. 'We'll find out before too long. Osorio and I haven't seen eye to eye for weeks so it was only a matter of time before we fell out for good. That's why I've been building the androids so slowly. I was aware that I'd made a bad decision throwing my lot in with him, so I kept finding ways to slow the process down.'

'But why did you team up with him in the first place?' Sienna asked.

'Because I'm a fool,' said Felso. 'And because I'm homesick and miss my family. I have a daughter on Galacdros who is about your age and I haven't seen her since she was seven years old. I'd like to be able to talk to her again, to apologise for tearing our family apart, and Osorio offered me the chance to get back there.'

They heard the sound of heavy boots pounding against the tunnel floor and seconds later a bullet ripped a chunk out of the wall close to Sophie's head. There was no time to discuss what they should do, they just turned and ran. Sophie sprinted through the poorly lit tunnels for all she was worth, moving so quickly over the rough damp earth that she almost lost her footing a couple of times. When they came to a fork in the tunnel, they were so closely packed together they were in danger of knocking each other over.

'Which way?' shouted Sienna.

'Left,' shouted Felso, 'no sorry, right, go right.'

But it was too late to correct the call. Sophie had already bolted into the left hand tunnel and Sienna and Felso into the right. They couldn't turn around to correct their mistake. The guards were too close behind them. They just had to keep on running and hope they could shake their pursuers off.

When Sophie realised she was on her own, the blood seemed to drain right out of her. She didn't think things could have got any worse, but now she was trapped underground with armed guards on her trail and she had been separated from the two people who were most likely to be able to get her out of there. At least the guards hadn't followed on after her. They seemed intent on chasing Professor Felso and had taken the right hand turn. But it was only a matter of time before the other guards realised she was on her own and set off to try to hunt her down.

CHAPTER 11

Sophie stopped and leaned against the wall, breathing heavily and looking left and right for any sign of the guards. It was cold and damp and she could see the roots of the trees poking through the soil above her head, a stark reminder that she was encased in the mass of earth under Crook's Wood. She tried not to think of the weight of it all or what would happen if one of the props that held it up were to give way. She already felt claustrophobic and frightened, and she just wanted to get out of there as soon as possible.

A host of thoughts rushed through her mind. Why did the guards follow Professor Felso and Sienna rather than chasing after her? Could Osorio have told them that she wasn't very important? If that were true and the guards were all chasing Sienna and Professor Felso, perhaps the exit into the wood wasn't guarded after all.

She took out the little book she'd bought that morning and started flipping through it to look for the map. It was quite difficult to read in the flimsy light, but eventually she found the map and flattened the book out to get a better look at it.

At first it looked like a tangle of snaking tunnels and it was difficult to make any sense of it. Her biggest problem was that she didn't know where she was on the map so it was hard to use it to navigate. For all she knew she could be only a few feet away from one of the exits and seconds away from freedom. It was very frustrating. The map did show two exits which she assumed were the exit through the kitchen and the concealed exit in the wood, but it wasn't clear which was which. She decided the best thing to do was search the surrounding area to try to establish where she actually was.

There were lots of old discarded items littering the ground as she crept slowly forward. At one point she picked up a length of metal pipe that looked as if it could make a handy weapon. It was about an inch thick and the length of her forearm and would probably do some damage if she were to give it her full force. Of course this assumed she could actually bring herself to use it in the first place. Landing a blow in karate against an evenly matched opponent was one thing, but could she crash a metal pipe into someone's head? Hopefully it wouldn't come to that but she took the metal pipe with her anyway.

Every bend and corner was approached with fear and apprehension. She felt like she was trapped inside a monstrous computer game where the consequences of losing were much too awful to contemplate. Somewhere in this vast tangle of tunnels, machines were hunting for her intent on doing her harm, but unlike most computer games she only had one life to lose.

It was deathly quiet. After a while she started walking on tip toes because the sound of her own footsteps seemed abnormally loud and she didn't want to give her position away. Even her breathing seemed unnatural and noisy. But then she heard the sound of other footsteps, and they were coming in her direction. A cold sweat enveloped her.

The footsteps were coming from a right hand turn up ahead, and Sophie was suddenly overcome by the urge to turn and run. It was a struggle to stay on top of it. She knew she was no match for the guards, but she also knew she couldn't keep hiding in these tunnels forever. At some point she may have to fight her way out and right now she had the metal pipe and the element of surprise.

Eventually her curiosity got the better of her. She tentatively poked her head around the corner and the sight she was greeted with made her heart leap with joy. It was Sienna. She wanted to run towards her and hug her in relief but at the last minute she remembered that there could be two Siennas out in the tunnels, Sienna and her android double.

So which one was this? Sophie was caught between euphoria and despair.

There wasn't much time to think about it. Whichever Sienna it was, she was only about fifty feet away and would arrive at any second. Sophie's heart was beating so fast she thought it might burst out of her chest. She wondered if she could establish a telepathic link. Was there time? She closed her eyes and tried to focus her attention, but her mind was racing so much it was hard to stop the stream of thoughts that were flashing in and out of her consciousness.

The footsteps were getting closer. She couldn't afford to let the android see her first. It was probably under orders to kill her. But what if she guessed wrong and attacked her friend? This was all such a nightmare.

Taking a deep breath, she tried to focus her mind

again. There was only a second or two left and she was desperate for some sort of sign. And then she picked up a strong image of Sienna crouching down in a tunnel with Professor Felso crouching by her side. Was this really a message from Sienna or just wishful thinking on her part? She didn't know. She couldn't be sure.

The footsteps were almost upon her. Had she established a telepathic link? Could she take a chance? Her mind was in a total panic. She knew she had to jump one way. It was decision time. Now!

When the footsteps reached the corner, Sophie brought the metal pipe crashing down onto Sienna's head. The force of the blow was so immense it knocked her backwards several feet sending her clattering back against the wall before crashing to the ground face down.

For a few seconds she just stood there staring blankly at the lifeless body of Sienna. What had she done? Had she just killed her friend? She felt frozen with fear and couldn't bring herself to take a closer look. And then her thoughts exploded with a sudden realisation.

The red bandana! This Sienna wasn't wearing a red bandana!

She took a step closer. There was no blood anywhere. And then she saw the wires sticking out of the side of

Sienna's head and the slight wisp of smoke she was giving off. It was the android. Her relief was so overwhelming she had to fight hard to hold back the tears. She'd guessed right, but it was a heart stopping moment, one that she never wanted to have to repeat.

After taking a few moments to pull herself together, she stepped across to the body of the android and rolled it over onto its back. Now that she was able to see it close up she could tell that it definitely wasn't Sienna. Pushing her hand inside the split in the android's head, she ripped out as many wires as she could, thankful that the skull wasn't made out of the same bulletproof material used on the android guards. She was determined to make sure this machine was totally deactivated. There could be no repeat of what she'd just been through.

Once the android had been taken out of the fight, she sat back and tried to think of a plan of action. There was no point in hanging around here. If she was going to find Sienna and Professor Felso she would need to get going. It was a nerve-racking search. There were so many twists and turns in the labyrinth of tunnels, she was terrified that at any moment she was going to walk straight into one of her pursuers.

Questions kept bubbling up in her mind. Where was

Sienna? Was she OK? What if the guards had already caught up with Sienna and Professor Felso and Sophie was now the only person they were hunting for? She longed to hear Sienna's voice, just to know that she was safe.

Then from somewhere in the tunnels she heard the voice of Garth, the android with the baseball cap. It sounded like he was barking orders at one of the other guards and she thought she heard the sound of a punch being thrown, followed by a scuffle and angry voices.

Casting all caution to the wind, she ran as fast as she could in the opposite direction, determined to get right away from this crazy, malfunctioning android. Every tunnel she turned into looked exactly the same as the last. It was like being caught up in a ghastly recurring nightmare. And when she turned the next corner the nightmare became a waking reality.

At the far end of the tunnel, snarling and growling and thumping its giant fist against the wall, she saw the monstrous demonic creature that had burst into the laboratory earlier. It was lumbering through the tunnel, clearly still enraged, and it was heading in her direction. What was she to do now? She couldn't go back the way she had come, yet she was gripped with terror at the thought of encountering this fearsome creature. She stood frozen to the spot as if her mind had suffered a short circuit.

CHAPTER 12

When the creature first saw Sophie it let out a terrifying roar, then lengthened its giant stride and barrelled down the tunnel towards her. By the time it was within touching distance, Sophie realised she had stopped breathing altogether. She pressed herself back against the wall trying to take in tiny breaths of air, but she was so stricken with fear she found it hard to move a muscle. The creature towered over her as if she was a small child. Its satanic red eyes seemed to drill right into her skull. Raising its gigantic arm, it reached out to touch her shoulder.

'Please, no,' she said, 'I'm a friend of Professor Felso.'

It moaned and snarled then opened its massive mouth to display two rows of jagged yellowing teeth. Sophie knew this creature could probably crush her with one of its gargantuan hairy hands. The metal pipe she was carrying would be useless against it. It would crush her like a grape. Her heart was racing. She could feel it hammering away inside her chest. She wanted to scream out and run as far away from this place as possible but she couldn't get her feet to move. They were rooted to the ground in terror.

Then just as the creature was about to grab hold of Sophie's shoulder, a small stone cracked against the side of its face, making it jerk its head to the side and howl with rage. As it wheeled around in fury, Sophie could hear heavy feet pounding against the earth and the sound of someone running at speed in their direction. A familiar voice barked out in a low whisper.

'Titan, no. Get back.'

She was so frozen with fear she couldn't move her head to look, but she prayed that she had recognised the voice of Professor Felso. The creature took a step back but Sophie still couldn't take her eyes off it. It was only when she felt the embrace of Sienna that she was able to take in her surroundings.

'Sophie, are you OK?' said Sienna. 'We've been searching for you everywhere.'

Sophie took a couple of deep breaths and relaxed into the reassurance of Sienna's embrace.

'Yes, I think I'm alright,' she said. 'I sure am glad to see you though.'

The creature had backed off now and was standing several feet away.

'I'm sorry that was so traumatic,' said Professor Felso. 'Titan would never hurt you though.'

It was comforting to hear him say the words but she was still shaking from the trauma of her experience.

'I'm OK now,' she said, trying to pull herself together, 'but we need to get away from here. I heard some guards talking further down the tunnel and one of them was that guard with the baseball cap. It sounded like they were having an argument and I think they ended up getting in a fight.'

'Oh no,' said Felso, 'it's starting to get out of control. If it's attacking the other androids then there's no telling what it might do.'

Before anyone could respond, two of Osorio's guards appeared at the far end of the tunnel. On catching sight of Felso and the girls, one of them raised his gun and fired a shot, hitting Felso square in the chest. He stumbled back against the wall, his eyes wide in shock, and slumped to the ground.

When the creature realised Professor Felso had been

hit, it let out a deafening cry of anger and rushed towards the guards, eating up the ground with its massive strides. As it bore down upon them, the guards managed to get off a few more shots but the bullets just bounced off the creature's chest, barely making an impact.

Despite the strength and agility of the guards they were no match for Titan. It smashed into them with its massive fists and battered them back against the wall. Undeterred, the guards leapt back into the fray and soon the three of them were a tangled mess of wrestling, bouncing against the walls of the tunnel as each side tried to get the upper hand. When they barged into one of the large posts that supported the beam above their heads, lumps of earth cascaded down on top of them. It looked as if the tunnel could collapse at any minute.

Just as Titan appeared to be getting the upper hand, another guard appeared on the scene. It was Garth, the malfunctioning android. Sophie watched in horror as he ran towards the fight laughing maniacally and carrying a small axe in his hand. He leapt into the fray wielding the axe, hacking at anyone and everything he could reach. The axe ripped into the creature's neck and it wobbled for a moment, letting out a low moan. Some vital connection in its circuits must have been affected and it seemed to lose some of its power.

Kneeling by Professor Felso's side, Sophie watched in horror while further down the tunnel the creature tried in vain to regain the upper hand. It was struggling to contain the guards' onslaught, and it seemed to realise it was fighting a losing battle. As Garth continued to hack away with the small axe, Titan looked across at Professor Felso lying injured on the ground then lifted up its massive arm and grabbed hold of the huge beam that propped up the earth above their heads.

Snarling and growling, it put all of its immense strength into one final effort and with a mighty heave it wrenched the beam out of position, bringing tons of earth crashing down onto the battle that was raging underneath. Titan and the guards were totally buried as an avalanche of soil and tangled roots collapsed on top of them.

The earthfall completely buried Titan and the guards and sent shockwaves through the tunnel, causing earth to start falling all around Professor Felso and the girls. Sophie looked at the mass of earth at the far end of the tunnel. Only a few minutes ago she had been frozen with fear in the presence of Titan, yet this colossal creature had just sacrificed itself to save Professor Felso and in doing so had saved the girls' lives as well.

She turned to Professor Felso. He was badly injured but he was smiling and a little tearful.

'Loyalty,' he said. 'I've been working on that for years. If only it was as easy to programme it into humans.'

He coughed and closed his eyes, trying to deal with the burning pain in his chest.

'Can you stand up?' said Sienna. 'We should get you away from here. We need to get you to a doctor.'

Felso tried to move but slumped back and shook his head.

'No,' he said, 'it's too late for that.'

He coughed sharply again and grimaced with the pain.

'There's something you'll need to know if you're going to be able to defeat Osorio,' he said, as the girls knelt beside him. 'They plan to take over.'

'Who does?' Sophie asked, 'Osorio and the guards?'

'No, it's much more serious than that,' Felso answered. 'There's a group of them, prominent people in this country. They have a secret society and they plan to take over.'

'Is Harry Jacobs one of them?' Sienna asked.

Professor Felso was finding it difficult to speak. His breath was very short and his eyes were only half open.

'I don't know,' he said, eventually. 'Osorio never told me who they were. But they intend to seize power, and they're going to start by trying to get rid of the Prime Minister.'

'The Prime Minister?' said Sophie. 'He's visiting the town this afternoon.'

'Yes,' said Professor Felso, 'and if Osorio has his way he won't be leaving alive. One of the androids has been programmed to assassinate him as he's walking around the town.'

'But why?' said Sophie in astonishment.

'It's part of a plan to put one of their people into the top job.'

He closed his eyes again and coughed roughly.

'And there are other androids as well,' he said. 'Watch out for…'

He coughed again and gritted his teeth.

'Please don't try to talk Professor,' said Sienna, 'we need to get you to a doctor.'

Felso didn't answer. He had lost consciousness and was barely breathing.

'Oh no,' said Sophie, trying to stop herself from

crying. 'We have to get him out of here. I'm sure that between us we could carry him. He can't weigh that much, he's no bigger than I am.'

They heard a frantic scratching and scraping sound coming from the pile of earth. Seconds later they could hear the voice of Garth. Somehow he had managed to survive the earthfall and he was now scratching away at it trying to find a way through. He was shouting about Professor Felso and the girls and what he intended to do when he caught up with them. He sounded insane.

Sienna bent down and tried to pick up the professor. He felt limp and heavy. She grabbed his wrist and looked for a pulse. When she couldn't find one she looked at Sophie and shook her head.

'I think we've lost him,' she said, 'but at least before he died he saw Titan's show of loyalty.'

Garth's rants were becoming louder and more insane. Finally a small hole appeared in the side of the pile of earth and they saw the barrel of a handgun poking through. Instantly it fired off a shot, hitting the tunnel wall a few feet from them. It was time to go. They couldn't wait here any longer. They had to get as far away from this deranged android as possible.

CHAPTER 13

Sophie felt terrible leaving Professor Felso behind but they really didn't have any choice. Garth had now become obsessed with finding them and the other androids were clearly under orders to shoot on sight. The girls knew they had to find a spot where they could regroup and think of a plan and, after a few minutes, they came to a tunnel that was cordoned off by a barrier. It was gloomy and dark and looked as if it had been abandoned long before any of the lighting had been installed.

Sienna took the small flashlight out of her pocket, turned it on and pointed it into the darkness. It didn't look any different to the rest of the tunnels but for the lack of lights.

'Let's have a look down here,' she said. 'It may be the one place they don't think of looking for us.'

Sophie wasn't convinced. It was obvious that nobody had been down there in ages. There were cobwebs hanging from the roots that poked through the earth and a smell of mould and decay filled the air. But Sienna was already on the move. She pulled aside the barrier and stepped into the tunnel.

At first they couldn't work out why the barrier was in place, but after they'd been walking for a while they came across a spot where several planks of wood had been laid across the ground. They stopped in front of them and Sienna lifted up one of the planks.

'I know what this is,' she said. 'It's an old well. Professor Felso told me about it when you got separated from us earlier. He thought we might be able to lure some of the androids down here and set a trap for them.'

'What sort of trap?' said Sophie.

'Well, there's supposed to be an old sheet of canvas around here somewhere.'

She shone the flashlight around, and a little further down they spotted a sheet of canvas that was folded neatly against the wall.

'Felso thought we could take away the planks of wood then spread the canvas over the top of the well to make it look like solid ground. It's so dark in here he thought the guards wouldn't notice what's happening under their feet, particularly if they were chasing us. Apparently, androids don't think they just act, so it won't occur to them that there's anything sinister about the canvas and as soon as they step on it they'll be gone.'

'But how are we supposed to lure them down here?' said Sophie.

Sienna thought for a minute.

'I'm not sure. Let's set the trap first, then we can worry about that.'

They hauled the planks of wood off the well to reveal a large hole about five feet in diameter. Next, they spread the canvas out on the ground to flatten it out as much as they could. Fortunately, it wasn't very thick and the creases fell out quite easily. Finally, they stretched the canvas over the top of the well and smoothed it out to ensure it was totally flat, taking care to cover the edges with loose earth. Once the trap had been set they had to admit it had a pretty good chance of working.

'Well, whatever happens,' said Sophie, 'it will definitely protect us from anyone coming towards us from the entrance of the tunnel. Now we can explore the rest of it without worrying that someone might be creeping up behind us.'

'You know, for a twelve-year-old schoolgirl you make a pretty good agent,' said Sienna, smiling at her.

Sophie returned her smile. Despite the perilous situation they were in, it felt good to receive a compliment and have a bit of light relief.

'By the way,' said Sophie. 'I picked up that book this morning and it does have a map in the back. I tried to use it to navigate when we got separated earlier but I couldn't quite make out where I was.'

She handed the book to Sienna who studied the map for a moment. She rotated it a few times and frowned, trying to remember which way they'd come to the well.

'Oh hang on, you don't think that little blob could be the well, do you?' said Sophie, pointing at the map.

'Oh yes, I suppose it might be,' said Sienna. 'But if it is, then according to the map, this tunnel is a dead end.'

'Oh no,' said Sophie. 'So what do we do now?'

Sienna was about to answer when they heard the barrier being moved at the mouth of the tunnel followed by the sound of footsteps. They peered around the bend and saw one of the guards pulling the barrier back into position and walking a short distance into the tunnel.

'Excellent timing,' Sienna whispered. 'Keep walking my friend. We've got a nice little surprise for you down here.'

The guard seemed hesitant about venturing in any further. He shone his flashlight into the murky depths but was unmoved by what he saw. Worried that he was about to turn and go back the way he had come, Sienna allowed her flashlight to flicker slightly to attract his attention. The guard stiffened and looked intently at the spot where he thought the light had come from, but after staring at it for a few seconds he turned and started to walk back towards the mouth of the tunnel. Sienna knew they couldn't allow that to happen. She picked up a rock from the floor and flung it as hard as she could in his direction. It bounced noisily off the wall then clattered across the ground before coming to a rest.

'Quick Sophie, run,' she shouted, as she and Sophie darted around the bend.

On hearing the noise, the guard spun around and sprinted towards them like a heat-seeking missile. They peered around the bend and watched as he got nearer and nearer to the well, praying that in the dim light he wouldn't see the canvas spread across the ground. And they weren't to be disappointed. He was moving so fast when he stepped on the canvas that he didn't even notice what was beneath his feet.

There were no screams of terror as he plummeted

down towards certain destruction. That wasn't part of his programme. He seemed to accept his fate quite calmly. It was as if someone had dropped a laptop down the well.

The girls stayed silent for a few seconds, listening for the sound of him hitting the bottom of the well, but it never came. Finally they crept around the bend and made their way tentatively towards the well, but when Sienna shone her flashlight down into the darkness they were met by a terrifying sight. The guard was looking up at them manically, one hand gripping onto the top of the well while his other hand tried to grab hold of something to help him climb up.

When he saw the girls, he reached down with his free hand and drew his gun, but as he raised his arm again, Sienna kicked the gun out of his hand and sent it skittering across the tunnel, out of reach.

But the guard wasn't beaten yet. Before the girls had time to move back, he reached up and grabbed hold of Sophie's ankle. As he tried to drag himself back up to ground level he was slowly pulling her forward into the well. She gasped and clung onto a large root that was hanging out of the wall, but she couldn't stop herself sliding slowly towards disaster.

Sienna knew she had to take swift action. She grabbed the metal pipe that Sophie had left leaning against the tunnel wall and repeatedly slammed it down onto the guard's wrist, desperately trying to break his grip on Sophie's ankle. It barely made a dent.

By now the guard had managed to find a foothold and his head and shoulders were becoming visible above the ground. As he started to haul himself up, Sienna jabbed her heel roughly into his face causing him to lose his grip on the top of the well and tumble backwards into the blackness.

Now he just had hold of Sophie's ankle and his weight was pulling her closer and closer to the edge. She could feel the earth crumbling beneath her feet. Then suddenly it collapsed under her, and with a yelp of terror she slipped over the side into the darkness. Sienna lurched at her frantically and just managed to grab hold of her arm, slowing Sophie down long enough for her to grip onto the top of the well with her other hand.

For a few seconds they dangled there. Sophie was desperately hanging onto Sienna's hand while her other hand gripped the top of the well. Further down, the guard was clinging onto the ankle of Sophie's boot. It had all happened so quickly Sophie barely had time to think. She closed her eyes and prayed that Sienna would be able to hold on.

Below her, the guard was frantically trying to get his other hand onto her boot as he swung to and fro like a pendulum. She knew she had to find a way to shake him off but it was taking all her concentration just to stop herself plummeting down into the well with him. In an effort to break his grip, she jammed the heel of her other boot down onto his hand, but without any luck. She tried again much more forcefully, then again and again. The heel of her boot was scraping against her shin as she repeatedly slammed her foot down but she was so terrified by her predicament she was impervious to the pain.

Above her, Sienna was finding it difficult to hold the combined weight of Sophie and the guard and was beginning to slide dangerously close to the edge. Again and again Sophie slammed her heel down onto the guard's hand but she couldn't budge it. Then just as she was beginning to think she couldn't hold on any longer, her heel crashed against the inside of her boot, loosening up the zip, and the guard tumbled away towards the bottom of the well carrying her boot down with him. Seconds later they heard him hit the bottom with a thud.

It didn't come a moment too soon for Sienna. She had been teetering dangerously close to the edge of the well and couldn't have held on much longer. Gathering together her last reserves of energy, she hauled Sophie up out of the darkness and they both collapsed onto the earthy tunnel floor. The relief the girls felt was immense. They were both breathing hard and it was a minute or so before either of them could speak. Eventually Sienna exhaled loudly and looked across at Sophie.

'Are you OK?' she asked.

'I think so,' Sophie answered. 'I'd be happier if I was still wearing two boots though.'

Sienna sat up, crawled over to the well and shone her flashlight into the darkness. It wasn't possible to see all the way to the bottom but, judging by how long it took the guard to hit the ground, it was definitely a long way down.

'Well, that's reduced the odds a little,' she said, crawling back to where Sophie lay. 'Osorio said Felso had supplied him with eight guards so far. Getting rid of this one brings that down to seven, and I'm sure poor old Titan took out another two when it pulled that support beam down. So that means that there are just five left.'

'And I got rid of the android Sienna earlier,' said Sophie.

'Wow, how did you do that?' Sienna asked.

'I smashed it on the head with that metal pipe. It was horrible. I had to make a split second decision whether it was the android or you.'

'What made you guess right?'

'I tried to focus my mind to see if I could make a telepathic link with you, and I got a distinct image of you and Professor Felso crouching down in the tunnels.'

'And that's exactly the message I was sending to you,' said Sienna. 'You see, you can do this. You just have to put in a lot more practice.'

'To be honest,' said Sophie, 'for a moment I thought I'd got it wrong. I thought I'd killed you. It was horrible.'

'That's why it's so important to practice,' said Sienna. 'At the moment you're really just guessing but with a little more practice you'll be able to act with certainty.'

Sophie knew that Sienna was right but it was hard to believe she could actually read other people's thoughts. An image flashed into her mind of android Sienna's crumpled body laying on the ground and she thanked her lucky stars she'd guessed correctly. The alternative was just too horrible to contemplate.

'What do you think Professor Felso meant when he was warning us about other androids?' said Sienna.

'I don't know,' Sophie answered. 'You don't think Osorio has an army of them somewhere else do you?'

'Let's hope not,' said Sienna. 'An army of deranged androids is the last thing I want to come across.'

She shone the flashlight further down the tunnel looking for the gun she had kicked out of the guard's hand. Once she had located it, she tucked it into her belt then crawled back to rejoin Sophie.

'So, what do we do now?' said Sophie.

Sienna took out the little book and shone her flashlight at the map.

'We should try to get to one of these exits before the rest of the guards find us,' she said. 'Let's work our way towards this point here. It could be the exit into Crook's Wood.'

'Didn't Professor Felso say the exit into the wood is likely to be heavily guarded?' said Sophie.

'Maybe it is,' Sienna answered, 'but now we have a gun. And let's face it, we don't really have any other alternative.'

CHAPTER 14

They hauled the planks of wood back over the top of the well then made their way to the mouth of the tunnel. In the improved lighting, Sienna studied the little book again and tried to memorise the route to the exit into Crook's Wood.

'I'm assuming this point here is the exit we're looking for,' she said, pointing at a spot on the map. 'From where we are right now it doesn't seem to be that far away.'

As Sienna studied the map, Sophie noticed some movement at the far end of the main tunnel and her heart sank. It was Garth and he was coming in their direction. They seemed to be stumbling from one crisis to another. She grabbed Sienna's arm and dragged her back inside the disused tunnel.

'We're going to have to do something about him,'

said Sienna. 'He's become obsessed with tracking us down and he's so much faster than us.'

She took out the gun she had picked up by the well.

'Do you remember what Professor Felso said about the androids' knees?'

'Yes,' said Sophie. 'He said it was their weak spot.'

'I wonder if a bullet to the knee would slow him down a bit. If it did it would give us a much better chance of getting out of here.'

'Are you suggesting we try it now?'

'Why wait?' Sienna answered.

Sophie wasn't so sure. She had just had one narrow escape. She didn't want to get involved in another life or death situation.

'But what if it doesn't slow him down?' she said. 'We'll have given our position away. We'll be sitting ducks.'

'We've got to do something, Sophie,' said Sienna, 'otherwise it's just a matter of time before they track us down.'

She crept forward to the tunnel entrance and peered around the corner. Garth was moving towards them, mumbling away insanely to himself.

'Those girls are going to be sorry when Garth finds

them,' he kept saying. 'Garth is going to make them suffer.'

Sienna knew that her first shot would need to be decisive. This had to be a direct hit. There would be no second chances. Crouching down low, she took careful aim for several seconds, waiting for the right moment to strike. Sophie found the tension unbearable. Why was she letting Garth get so close? What was she waiting for? Eventually Sienna squeezed off a shot. The bullet ripped a lump out of Garth's knee, sending him clattering against the wall and careering around the tunnel before he collapsed to the ground with a thud.

It sent him into a rage. Shouting angrily, he tried to get to his feet but when he did he just toppled over again.

'Garth isn't happy,' he kept shouting. 'You girls are going to pay for this.'

He struggled to his feet but he was walking very unsteadily, like a man with a badly torn muscle in his leg, and by the time he managed to steady himself the girls had already gone.

They wandered through the tunnels for what seemed like an eternity. It felt to Sophie like they were stuck inside a massive underground maze with no way out. She limped along by Sienna's side, wincing whenever her bootless foot stepped on a sharp stone. She was cold and hungry and beginning to doubt whether Sienna had the slightest idea where the exit was.

But when they reached the next corner, they could see a bright light a little further down and an opening into a larger space beyond it. They stopped and pressed themselves against the wall, aware that this area could be heavily populated by guards.

'I think I know where we are,' Sophie whispered.

She took the map back and studied it for a few seconds.

'I think that's the laboratory where we were held earlier,' she said, pointing towards the bright light.

They could hear voices. Osorio was barking instructions at someone and they heard the sound of someone dragging something across the ground. When they peered around the corner they could see it was Garth dragging his foot as he walked.

Sophie didn't know how much longer she could trail around underground in these dank tunnels, hoping not to run into one of the guards. Perhaps it was time to make a stand. The thought didn't fill her with a great deal of joy, but she knew that sooner or later they were going to have to fight their way out. Sienna checked the magazine in her gun. Only three cartridges left.

Inside the laboratory, Osorio was talking to someone in a low voice. He stopped for a moment in mid-sentence, thinking he could hear voices coming from somewhere nearby, then, listening intently, he slowly stepped through the door and out into the tunnel.

'I know you're out here somewhere, Sienna,' he shouted. 'And I know you can probably hear me. You and your idiotic friend have messed things up for me once again and this time I'm going to make sure you don't get another chance.'

He walked up and down for a few seconds waiting for a response, but none was forthcoming. The girls crouched in the darkness listening to the sound of Osorio's boots crunching against the ground. They were sure he was armed and they couldn't be sure how many of the guards were with him. Their only hope was to bide their time and hope to take him by surprise.

'You know you're just like your father,' Osorio continued. 'Determined to defend a system that serves those who are in power while the rest of our world stagnates. You could be a powerful warrior. You could lead our world to a glorious future, but instead you've pledged your allegiance to those who wish to protect their own interests. Your father used to dream of a better world, but now he is weak and complacent and part of that self-interested establishment.'

Sophie could see that Sienna was finding it difficult to keep quiet. She reached across and grabbed Sienna's arm then shook her head vigorously, imploring her not to respond.

'It doesn't matter though,' said Osorio. 'Soon it will be all over for you. I wasn't stupid enough to expect loyalty from Felso and I took a few precautions to make sure I would be able to cover my tracks should the need arise. I hope you and your little friend enjoy your last few moments together. It is fitting that your life will end up as pathetic and meaningless as your father's.'

Sienna couldn't stay quiet any longer. She stepped around the corner and fired a shot, narrowly missing Osorio's head and causing him to dive back into the safety of the laboratory. But Garth didn't move. He just stood there laughing at Sienna, looking as if he'd totally lost his mind.

'We've got them now,' he shouted. 'We've got them now. You girls are going to suffer for wasting Garth's time, making him chase around underground for so long.'

He started limping forward, grunting and muttering with every step he took. Before ducking back around the corner, Sienna fired another shot. It ripped against the side of his damaged knee but this time he didn't overbalance. He just tottered for a moment before steadying himself again. Then he kept limping towards her.

Only one cartridge left. Sienna knew she would have to make this one count. Garth was now only about thirty feet away, limping towards the corner and laughing like a maniac. Sienna had faced many moments like this during her training but this was the first time she had ever put that training into practice. It was time to find out whether she had the right stuff.

She stepped around the corner, crouched down low and steadied herself to take aim for the final time. When Garth saw her he became even more hysterical and frantic. He was now totally out of control. Slowly and gently Sienna fired the last cartridge. When it entered Garth's open mouth and smashed upwards into his skull, the power circuits inside his head exploded with a puff of smoke and a sudden flash of light. He paused for a moment, swaying slightly and staring wildly all about him. There was a moment when it seemed he might keep coming towards them, then he stumbled and crashed against the wall and his head burst into a raging ball of flames.

Sienna retreated behind the wall as the flaming figure of Garth careered around the tunnel firing his gun randomly as he barged drunkenly against the walls. Finally, he collapsed with a resounding clunk onto the tunnel floor and lay there twitching as the fire consumed him. The girls breathed a massive sigh of relief.

They heard the sound of footsteps moving quickly away from the area. Before too long it turned to the sound of someone running. Deprived of the support of his demented side kick, Osorio had obviously fled.

What were they to do now? The smoke from the burning body of Garth was making their eyes stream, but Sienna wanted to get closer to see if she could retrieve her knife and check whether his gun had any cartridges left. They waited for a few minutes to let the intensity of the fire die down then walked cautiously towards Garth's flaming carcass.

But before they could get within a few feet of him, the tunnels were rocked by a deafening explosion. The force of it was so immense it knocked them both to the ground, engulfing them in dust and other small fragments of debris. Seconds later there was another explosion of equal strength. They covered their eyes and mouth to keep out the dust but it was as if they were in a fog. The tunnel was a mass of swirling dust and one of the support beams further down looked as if it was about to give way. Sophie knew they had to get out of there, and quickly.

CHAPTER 15

Struggling to her feet and coughing up dust, Sophie wiped the dirt and grime from her face. It was hard to breathe and her ears were ringing from the ferocity of the blasts, but she was relieved to see that Sienna had survived unscathed. They were just beginning to gather themselves when there was another massive explosion, this time it came from the far end of the tunnels. Initially it didn't seem to have as much impact as the others, but within a few seconds it wasn't just dust they had to contend with. Water was flooding into the tunnel and it was moving with quite a force.

'The lake,' said Sophie. 'He must have blown a hole in the wall next to the lake.'

Before they had a chance to decide what to do, they were hit by a tidal wave of water. It knocked them off their feet and swept them down the tunnel like leaves in a rain storm. The explosion had also taken out the lights so they were in total darkness, bumping along against the tunnel walls and desperately trying to keep their heads above the water. Sophie felt Sienna reach out and take her by the hand.

'Give me your hand, Sophie,' she spluttered through the water. 'We have to make sure we stay together, it'll give us a much better chance of surviving.'

Soon the water level had almost reached the roof of the tunnel and at times their heads were banging against the rough earth as they were swept along by the power of the current. When the surge started to ease a little, Sophie felt Sienna tug on her arm and pull her over towards the tunnel wall.

'I've got hold of some sort of rail,' she said. 'Hold onto this, it'll give us a chance to catch our breath.'

Sophie grabbed hold of the rail and hung on for dear life. She was coughing and spluttering and gratefully trying to breathe in without swallowing any more of the water.

'I wonder if the flashlight still works,' said Sienna.

She took the light out of her pocket and flipped the switch. Miraculously, it still threw out a sharp light. Sophie could see that they were directly underneath the exit to the kitchen. Unfortunately, the steps had been blown apart by the explosion and the exit was quite a way above them.

Now that they had stopped being battered by the current, the girls became aware of how cold the water was. They were shivering and their teeth were starting to chatter. Sophie knew they wouldn't last too long in this temperature.

'We've got to get out of this water,' she said. 'There must be somewhere around here that's above the water line.'

When Sienna shone the light around, they saw a section of wall that had collapsed creating a mound of rubble that might be able to hold their weight. They swam over to it and carefully climbed on.

'It seems quite solid,' said Sienna, 'but we won't be able to stay here for long.'

She shone the light up to where the exit to the kitchen had once been. Now that the staircase had been blown away it was difficult to see how they could possibly get up to it. Their only chance of escape may be to swim to the exit into the wood and hope it was still open, but first they would have to find out how to get there.

'Do you still have that map?' she asked.

Sophie took the little book out of her pocket. It was dripping wet and the pages were all stuck together, but they managed to find the map and Sienna shone the light onto it so they could study the tangle of tunnels. Once she was familiar with the layout, she scanned the surrounding area with the flashlight then looked back at the map.

'Well, based on the pattern of tunnels we can see leading away from here, we must be at this exit,' she said, pointing at the map. 'So this spot over here has to be the exit into the wood.'

'True, but how are we going to get to it?' said Sophie.

'I'm afraid we might have to swim underwater,' Sienna answered.

She knew that an underwater swim in the dark would be the last thing Sophie wanted to do, but she also knew they couldn't just stay where they were and hope someone came along to rescue them. The chances of anyone discovering them were slim, and by the time they did the girls may have succumbed to the cold.

'Isn't there any way we could make it up to the kitchen?' said Sophie, staring up at the exit high above them.

'It's twenty feet up, Sophie. If the tunnels weren't flooded we could have looked around for something to use as a climbing frame, but we're not likely to find anything like that now. I know you're not keen on the underwater swim but it could be our only way out of here. Let me go and take a look around. It might be closer than we think.'

'But you might not find a spot where you can come up for air. You could get trapped down there.'

'Well, fortunately this is one of the things we train for at The Academy,' said Sienna, smiling at her. 'We have to do a series of underwater swims, and in one of them I held my breath for four minutes and thirty seven seconds. And I think I could have held on even longer.'

'Presumably you'll have to take the light with you,' said Sophie, terrified by what Sienna's departure would actually mean.

'I'm afraid so,' Sienna answered. 'I shouldn't be gone for long though. I don't think it's that far, judging by this map anyway.'

Sienna studied the map for a few more seconds, memorising the route she would need to take, then took several deep breaths and prepared to depart.

'I'll try not to be too long,' she said, leaning across to

give Sophie a hug. Then she stepped from the mound of earth and plunged into the icy water.

The next second she had disappeared, and Sophie was left alone and in total darkness. It was chilling to be in such a perilous position. Only a few hours earlier she had been on her way back from the bookshop, looking forward to meeting Sienna for tea and cake in the cafe. The android Sienna had been so lifelike. No wonder it was able to lure her into Osorio's trap. She thought about her mum visiting the town hall that afternoon and Osorio's plot to assassinate the Prime Minister. What if her mum was in the vicinity at the time of the attack and the android wasn't a very good shot? What if she was hit by a stray bullet? Androids are only machines after all. Somehow, she had to get out of there and warn someone about the attack.

It was cold and lonely waiting for Sienna's return. She wanted to stay strong and work with Sienna to get them both out of there, but she knew that her resolve was fading fast. Ever since Sophie first met Sienna at the Grand Hotel in Bramlington Bay, she had been fascinated and inspired by her. That's what the running after school and the karate classes were all about. She thought Sienna was truly amazing, the most impressive girl she'd ever met, and she wanted to be just like her. But that's an easy thing to dream of when you're living in a cosy, affluent town like Hampton Spa. The reality of her current situation was completely different.

It was a struggle to stay on top of her emotions. She was afraid that when Sienna returned they would have to swim underwater to an exit somewhere out there in the darkness, but Sophie wasn't sure she would be able to do it. She had always suffered a little from claustrophobia, and now she knew what lay ahead the panic was starting to build up inside her.

Just when it looked like things couldn't get any worse, a squeaking and chattering sound started coming from close by. It stopped for a few seconds but then she heard it again, and this time it was coming from more than one place. If things had looked bleak a moment ago this had taken it to a completely different level. Now she was going to have to deal with rats. She put her fist in her mouth and bit on the knuckle, trying not to let the fear overtake her. Where was Sienna? She should have been back by now. Sophie wasn't sure how much more of this she could take.

Something small and furry brushed against her leg. She let out a scream and lashed out at it with her arm then started to overbalance in panic, just stopping herself from toppling into the water. She had to stay calm, it was her only hope. There were quite a few of them but because of the total blackout she had no idea where they actually were. Something scuttled across the mound of earth she was sitting on and she lashed out again. This time she was sure she made contact. It was followed by a splashing sound as whatever she had struck hit the water. The squeaking and chattering became more pronounced and something started scrabbling at her boot. She leapt to her feet in a panic.

'Go away,' she screamed. 'Get away from me, all of you.'

On hearing her voice, the squeaking and chattering seemed to reach a crescendo. Tears were forming in her eyes, and her body was rigid with fear as she stood on the mound of earth waiting for the next invasion. And then inexplicably the noise subsided and everything was silent again. Shaking uncontrollably, and trying not to overbalance, she stood on the mound of earth, unable to bring herself to sit down again.

Another few minutes passed and still there was no sign of Sienna. What if she had miscalculated and taken a wrong turn? She may be stuck somewhere right now, desperately searching for a place to get her head above the water. Or she may have tried to squeeze through a small gap and be trapped, unable to wriggle free. If that was the case, then Sophie could be stuck down here forever.

CHAPTER 16

She was awoken from her thoughts when she saw a faint flickering of light in the darkness, then with a loud splash Sienna's head burst through the water, gasping for air. As the flashlight lit up the area, Sophie took hold of her outstretched hand and hauled her out of the water onto the mound of earth. She was clearly very cold and tired and was shivering so much that Sophie put her arms around her, pulling her in close in an attempt to warm her up. Finally, after a few moments, through chattering teeth, Sienna was able to talk.

'I've found it,' she said, still breathing hard.

'Do you mean the exit into the wood?' said Sophie.

'Yes,' Sienna answered. 'It's not that far but most of it is an underwater swim.'

'I was worried that you might have got stuck somewhere,' said Sophie. 'You've been gone for such a long time.'

'Yes, sorry about that,' said Sienna. 'I had to work a bit to make sure the exit was big enough for us to get through. I had to dive several times then come back up for air. Just let me warm up a bit, then we can get out of here.'

They sat in silence for several seconds. In the light that was thrown out by the flashlight, Sophie could now see that the water level had reached the top of the tunnels. If they hadn't found this area below the kitchen exit they would certainly have perished by now. There was no sign of the rats. They seemed to have moved on. She visualised what it would be like to swim through a dark tunnel in the cold water and the thought of it was making her feel quite panicky.

'I'm not sure I can do this, Sienna,' she said, eventually. 'I get claustrophobic in enclosed spaces and I'm terrified of drowning.'

'I don't think we have much choice,' said Sienna. 'There isn't any other way out. We could sit here and hope somebody comes to the house to rescue us but that may not happen for several days, maybe even weeks. We're cold and wet now and during the night the temperature will drop a lot further. We have to take a chance and go for it.'

'Couldn't you swim to the exit into the wood then go back to the house and lower something down for me to climb up to the kitchen?' said Sophie.

'Too risky,' said Sienna. 'Osorio could have left some of the guards at the house and if they managed to get the better of me you may never get out of here.'

Sophie's heart sank. She knew that Sienna was right but that didn't make the thought of swimming underwater any more appealing. What if they didn't make it through to the wood and were trapped under the water forever? Their families would never find out what had happened to them. Tears started to run down her face.

'I can't do it, Sienna,' she said. 'There has to be another way out. I'm not good in situations like this.'

'Yes, you are,' said Sienna. 'You proved that on Kestrel Island. When you were staring down the barrel of Rupert Flynn's gun you were powerful and dignified, and I wouldn't have made it back to the mainland if it wasn't for your courage.'

'Yes, but this is different,' said Sophie. 'This is underwater, in an enclosed space in the dark.'

'Yes, but nobody is chasing after us trying to kill us, are they?' said Sienna. 'There are no armed guards hunting us down. This time it's us against the elements, and the choice we have to make is the same choice we make in every moment of our lives. Are we going to hide in the dark and hope the challenge we're facing goes away, or are we going to stand tall and live our lives with dignity and courage? The way we answer that question defines who we really are.'

'That's easy for you to say,' said Sophie, angrily. 'You've trained for this sort of thing all your life. I'm just an ordinary girl from Hampton Spa.'

'No, you're wrong,' said Sienna, defiantly. 'You're anyone you choose to be. If you want to cling to the safety of being dull and ordinary, that's your choice. But there's a warrior inside you that is brave and powerful and capable of achieving anything. To unleash that power all you have to do is face your fears and do what needs to be done.'

Sophie didn't respond. She sat and looked at her hands, not knowing what to say. But Sienna wasn't finished yet.

'If we never get out of here, then Osorio wins,' she said. 'I'm not going to allow that to happen.'

She sat and waited for Sophie to respond but it was a long wait. Eventually Sophie wiped the tears from her eyes and looked across at her.

'How far is it?' she asked.

'There are two sections,' said Sienna, 'and I've timed them both. For the first section you'll have to hold your breath for a count of thirty five. There's a spot where the tunnel bends and you can get your head above water to breathe again. Then the second section is a count of twenty eight but it's quite narrow.'

'How narrow?' Sophie asked, looking quite alarmed.

'We'll have to go through one at a time,' said Sienna.

Sophie bit her lip and stared at the water lapping onto her feet.

'So, thirty five seconds and twenty eight seconds,' she said, 'and maybe a twenty second break to take in more air.'

'Yes, that's about right,' said Sienna.

'We could be out of here in less than two minutes then.'

Sienna nodded and smiled at her, trying to give Sophie the time to come to her own decision.

'OK,' said Sophie, 'let's get it over with.'

Sienna smiled at her again and gave her a hug.

'Now, as it's so dark down there we're going to swim as a pair so we don't get split up,' she said. 'We'll hold hands and use our outside arm and our legs to propel ourselves forward. And when we first get into the water it will be freezing cold so we're not going to hang around. As soon as we're in, take hold of my hand, take a deep breath and we'll be heading for that tunnel over there.'

Sophie looked at the water once more and tried to quell the fear that was almost choking her. They took several deep breaths then plunged into the icy water. Despite having been warned in advance, Sophie wasn't ready for how cold it actually was. She gasped in shock and took several short breaths.

'Before we go under, get control of your breathing again,' said Sienna, treading water. 'Take another few deep breaths and then we'll go under.'

They linked hands and took several deep breaths.

'OK,' said Sienna, 'let's make this quick. On the count of three take a deep breath and duck under the water, and make sure that the only thing you're thinking about is how good it will feel when we're out.'

Sienna counted to three and they both took a huge breath then ducked their heads under the water. Keeping a tight grip on Sienna's hand, Sophie kicked her legs furiously as they swam towards the tunnel opening. She remembered that Sienna said it was a count of thirty five before there would be a chance to take another breath, so she started counting slowly. Nine, ten, eleven.

Even though the flashlight threw out a little light, the tunnel was bleak and eerie as they swam side by side through the darkness. Sophie was reminded of the TV programmes she had seen of salvage hunters exploring a sunken ship wreck. She comforted herself with the thought that at least they wouldn't have to deal with sharks or a giant squid. Eighteen, nineteen, twenty.

It was harder than she thought to hold her breath for this length of time and soon Sophie's lungs were starting to hurt. She tried desperately to focus her attention on counting, but there didn't seem to be any end in sight and she wasn't sure how much longer she could hold on. Was she counting too quickly? Thirty one, thirty two, thirty three. Surely they must be almost there.

The pain in her chest was now becoming unbearable, and she had to fight the urge to slowly let the air out of her lungs. Thirty nine, forty, forty one. What? Where is the stop that Sienna promised? Forty six, forty seven. She desperately wanted to ask Sienna what was going on but that was impossible. Maybe Sienna had decided to push on to the next spot and didn't have the chance to tell her. She had to exhale, she couldn't hold it any longer. Fifty, fifty one.

When Sienna dragged her up out of the water, it didn't come a moment too soon. She choked and spluttered and breathed all at the same time, grateful for the chance to ease the pressure on her lungs. They were in a small air pocket and it was tempting to stay a while longer, but the cold water was sapping her energy so she knew there was no time to hang around.

'Why did that take so long?' she gasped. 'I was counting to thirty five so I'd know how far we'd gone, but we went way past that.'

'Sometimes we count too quickly when we're in combat situations,' said Sienna. 'It's very hard to slow our minds down when our heart is pumping so fast. OK, are you ready for the next section?'

'Will it be as much fun as that?' said Sophie, trying to hide her fear.

'I'm afraid so. But it won't take quite as long.'

'Good. I've already had enough excitement for one day.'

'Now, when we get close to the exit,' said Sienna, 'the tunnel gets really narrow so we'll have to go in single file. You go first and I'll shine the flashlight ahead of me so you can see where you're going.'

'How narrow is it?' said Sophie.

'Well, there isn't room for us to swim normally so you'll have to have your arms out in front of you to pull yourself along.'

Sophie gulped. Just the thought of being in such an enclosed space filled her with terror.

'I'm not sure I can do this, Sienna,' she said. 'What if I panic when I'm in there?'

'I'm afraid this is one of those times when you have to get control of your mind,' Sienna answered. 'You have to control the thoughts that are going through your head and make sure you're only thinking about how good it will feel when you succeed. And besides, the only alternative is to go back the way we just came.'

Sophie inhaled and braced herself for what lay ahead. She knew there was no option but to carry on.

'How long will it take?'

'In normal time it's a count of twenty eight but in Sophie time about forty,' said Sienna, smiling at her. 'OK, on the count of three.'

They both took another deep breath and plunged under the icy water again. Up ahead, Sophie could just make out where the narrow part of the tunnel started. It had obviously collapsed after the explosion, but there was a small gap that was still supported by a cross beam and it looked just about big enough for them to get through. Eighteen, nineteen, twenty.

As they neared the small exit hole, Sophie was having second thoughts about going in first, but she was also worried that if she went in second she would have to hold her breath for a lot longer. Twenty five, twenty six.

But she didn't get a chance to give it any more thought. When they reached the gap Sienna drew Sophie's hand towards it and pushed her into the narrow space. Her lungs were now starting to hurt again and she desperately wanted to exhale. Thirty two, thirty three, thirty four. With her hands out in front of her, Sophie grabbed hold of the earth on either side of the gap and pulled herself along, but it was so cramped there was barely enough room for her to squeeze through. How was this section of the tunnel still standing? Could it have been so weakened by the explosion that the tiniest movement could now bring the whole thing crashing down on top of her? It seemed to go on forever as she desperately tried to pull herself towards the exit.

Then her heart leapt when she thought she could see a tiny speck of light. At first it was just a flicker that she hoped she hadn't imagined, but then she saw it again. This time it was more intense and it didn't disappear. It got bigger and brighter and suddenly her head was out of the water and she was gasping for air. She was so elated she forgot to keep moving until she could feel Sienna crashing into her feet.

The girls dragged themselves from the water and crawled out into the thicket of bushes, squinting in the afternoon light and gratefully taking the air into their lungs. The experience of the last few hours had been so intense it felt to Sophie like she had landed in a foreign country. This may have been the wood that bordered her home town but today it seemed wonderfully exotic and welcome. They fought their way through the tangle of bushes that surrounded the exit and collapsed onto the woodland floor, sprawling themselves out on their backs and staring up at the canopy of the trees. Sophie was soaking wet, exhausted and freezing cold, but she was still alive and she couldn't remember a time when she felt so happy and relieved.

CHAPTER 17

After lying on the ground for a few minutes, Sophie sat up and looked at her watch. Despite the time she had spent underwater it still seemed to be working. She looked across at Sienna.

'We have to let the police know the Prime Minister is in danger,' she said. 'He starts his walkabout in just over two hours.'

'We can't, Sophie,' said Sienna. 'I'm under orders not to reveal my identity to the authorities in your world. How would we explain to the police who Osorio is and how we know what his plans are?'

'But one of those guards is programmed to kill the Prime Minister, and my mum is going to be somewhere nearby. We can't just sit back and do nothing.'

'We're not going to sit back,' said Sienna. 'We're going to go into the town and find that assassin, just as soon as we've taken another look around Heath Grange.'

'Heath Grange!' said Sophie, staring at her in shock. 'You must be joking. We're lucky not to have been killed in those tunnels. Why put us straight back into danger?'

'In case you've forgotten,' said Sienna, trying to stay calm, 'I came to this world to find Osorio and reclaim The Orb. So before we leave, I have to find out whether he's still in that house.'

'But he's already tried to kill us twice and he's got an army of guards who are probably under orders to shoot us on sight. Surely the one person we don't want to come across right now is Osorio.'

'Sophie, this isn't a holiday for me. I'm working. I'm carrying out my orders as a member of The Elite. You know that. You've known that since the start.'

'But what if we get caught again?' Sophie shouted in exasperation. 'What if we don't get back to the town in time and the Prime Minister gets killed or, even worse, my mum? Why don't you think about someone else for once? You're always dragging me into these dangerous situations. It's a miracle I'm still alive.'

'Hey,' Sienna shouted back. 'I'm only here right now because I came out to Heath Grange to rescue you. So if anything, you dragged me into a dangerous situation.'

She stood up and stared out into the trees.

'I'm going to the house,' she said, looking anywhere but at Sophie. 'I'm sure you'll be able to find your way back to the town without me.'

Sophie knew she had gone too far. She was overcome with remorse, unable to believe what she had just said.

'Sienna, I'm sorry,' she said, as Sienna started to walk away. 'That came out all wrong. Honestly. I'm very grateful you tried to rescue me. If it wasn't for you I'd probably still be down in the tunnels. And you're right, we should check out Heath Grange before we go into the town. There's still plenty of time.'

'Are you quite sure?' said Sienna, still visibly bristling. 'I wouldn't want to drag you into any more dangerous situations.'

'Yes, I'm sure,' Sophie answered, feeling a little chastened.

In the heat of the moment all the emotion and fear that had built up in the tunnels had spilled out of Sophie. She was horrified that she had taken it out on Sienna. She trailed along after her wearing only one boot, thankful that the woodland floor was a lot less punishing than the tunnels.

When they reached the house it looked as if it had

been abandoned. There was no sign of Osorio or the guards anywhere. The front door was wide open and the car Sophie had travelled out to Heath Grange in was nowhere to be seen. They circled around to the back of the house and entered through the kitchen door.

Once inside, they found a large room just off the kitchen that Sophie assumed was Professor Felso's office. Some papers were strewn across a mahogany desk and various other items were dotted around the room, including a pair of leather boots that were sitting on a chair by the window.

'Professor Felso was so small that those boots might fit you,' said Sienna, still not looking at Sophie.

Sophie looked at the boots. Sienna was right. They could actually be her size.

'Oh no,' she said. 'I couldn't just take them without asking. That wouldn't be right.'

'Well, at least try them on,' Sienna snapped, 'otherwise you're going to have to limp back to the town with only one boot on.'

Sophie could tell that Sienna was still stinging from their earlier disagreement. She sat down and tried the boots on. As she did, Sienna rifled through some of the papers that were scattered across the desk.

'Wow, look at this,' she said, picking up one of the papers. 'It's a letter from James Masterson to Osorio telling him about an apartment block in Hampton Spa and giving details of where to pick up the keys.'

Sophie stood up and looked at the papers.

'I think I know that building,' she said. 'It's in the old town where all the cafes and bars are.'

'Maybe this is where Osorio has been staying while he's in Hampton Spa,' said Sienna. She folded up the letter and put it in her pocket then sifted through the rest of the papers, wondering what else she would find.

But the search came to an abrupt halt when they heard the sound of a car arriving outside the house and a door being slammed. When they looked out the window, they were horrified to see one of Osorio's guards walking quickly towards the kitchen door. There wasn't time to make a run for it. Their only option was to hide behind the large sofa in the corner and hope for the best.

Seconds later the guard entered the house and came straight into the office. After rummaging through the pile of papers on the desk, he went into a room at the front of the house then quickly up the stairs. As soon as they heard his footsteps pounding across the floor above them, the girls decided to make a break for it. They rushed out through the open front door, making for the safety of the trees. Just as they reached the edge of the wood, a window at the top of the house flew open and the sound of gunshots cracked through the air behind them.

As they ran full tilt into the heart of the wood, Sophie was glad she was still wearing the pair of boots she had borrowed from Professor Felso's office. Trying to run wearing only one boot could have slowed her down considerably, and even though they had a head start on the guard, she knew their advantage wouldn't last for long.

'We'll never outrun him,' said Sienna, panting hard and looking all around. 'Let's climb up that big tree over there. He's probably not programmed to look up.'

Sophie couldn't have disagreed more. She knew they would be hopelessly exposed if the guard saw them at the top of the tree, but after the argument they had a short while ago she didn't want to risk any more friction. As Sienna leapt onto the large oak tree, Sophie found a spot on the other side and quickly followed her up.

It was hard going scrabbling up the craggy bark. Sophie wasn't used to climbing trees and she found it terrifying to be up so high. Every time she released her grip to reach for something higher she felt vulnerable and anxious, but she knew she had to keep pushing forward to find a secure hiding place.

While focussing more on where she was putting her hands than on what was in front of her, she pushed her face through a large spider's web and let out a gasp of disgust. She had always been terrified of spiders and the thought that a web was on her face filled her with horror. She desperately wanted to reach down and wipe it off, but she was so far up the tree by now she couldn't bring herself to let go with either hand. Eventually they reached the seclusion of the top of the tree and Sophie could wipe her face clear of the web. It was a massive relief. At that very moment the guard appeared down below.

Perched in the thin branches at the top of the tree, the girls watched and waited, trying to keep perfectly still. They knew the slightest movement or sound could give them away and they couldn't be sure how sensitive the guard's hearing was.

After the horror of the climb, Sophie was desperately trying to calm herself down, but when she looked down at her arm the sight she was greeted with made her break out in a cold sweat. A large, fat spider was on the sleeve of her jacket, and it was slowly making its way up towards her elbow. Her whole body clenched and she could feel herself starting to shake. She knew she couldn't react. All she could do was watch the terrifying creature as it made its way slowly past her elbow and started moving up towards her shoulder. It was big and fat from a summer of feasting on the tiny creatures of the wood and it was getting closer and closer to her face.

With the guard still directly below them, Sophie bit her lip and tried to keep her nerve. The spider was now on her shoulder, heading for the open neck of her shirt. It was so close to her face that she thought she was going to throw up. Then out of the corner of her eye, she saw Sienna's hand moving very slowly towards her holding a loose branch. It reached Sophie just as the spider was crawling onto the collar of her shirt, and as it was about to step onto her neck, Sienna flicked at it with the branch and the spider flew noiselessly through the air, landing on the soft woodland floor below them.

Sophie exhaled as quietly as she could and her eyes darted across to look at Sienna. She was greeted with a smile and a nod of the head. Once again Sienna had saved her. Once again she was filled with remorse for her earlier comments. She smiled back at Sienna, grateful that her friend seemed to have forgiven her.

Down below, the guard decided he had seen enough. Wherever the girls were they obviously weren't anywhere near here, so he turned and started walking back towards the house. It was a few minutes before Sophie and Sienna were prepared to move. They sat in the tree and watched the guard slowly disappear into the distance, grateful that they hadn't been spotted and determined to make their good fortune pay.

'Right,' said Sienna, 'let's get into the town and find that assassin.'

CHAPTER 18

When they reached the town, it was swarming with police due to the extra security demanded for the visit of the Prime Minister. Sophie had never seen Market Square so busy. It was teeming with shoppers and sightseers. Some were there to see if they could catch a glimpse of the Prime Minister, perhaps even get a selfie with him to show to their grandchildren in years to come. Others were going about their normal daily business. Stallholders, businessmen, shop workers and traffic police, all trying to cope with the extra demands that the visit of a VIP creates.

The girls stood in the square and scanned the buildings opposite the town hall. They were all four storeys high and would be the perfect spot for a sniper to get off a few shots before making a getaway through the back streets. Someone was definitely up there, but it wasn't what they were expecting. Two armed police officers were standing watch on the roof, scouring the surrounding buildings for any signs of trouble.

'Well, I think they've got that covered,' said Sophie. 'It doesn't look like there's going to be a sniper attack.'

'In that case the assassin must already be here in the square,' said Sienna.

There were so many people squeezed into the area, the girls found it hard to see more than a few feet in front of them. If the assassin was already in position, it was going to be quite a job to find him. They ran over to a set of steps that led up to the entrance of a bank and from the top they had a much better view over the heads of the people.

At the other side of the square, Sophie could see the Prime Minister making his way through the crowd, shaking hands with people and waving to those who were hanging out of first floor windows. She could also see Will Starkey trailing after him, constantly trying to butt in to ask a question and constantly being pushed back by the security staff. So far, everything seemed quite normal.

Then her eyes were drawn to someone emerging from behind the town hall, moving briskly towards the Prime

Minister's entourage. At first she couldn't be sure because he was a long way away, but when she looked more closely she was certain she had spotted one of Osorio's guards.

'Sienna, look,' she said, pointing to the other side of the square. 'That man in the dark green jacket, walking past the cycle racks.'

When Sienna spotted him as well, they both knew what this meant. Osorio had planned a close up attack all along, and now they only had a few seconds to save the Prime Minister's life.

They bolted down the steps and out across the square, barging their way through the crowd in an attempt to get to the assassin. There were so many people milling around that it was difficult to make any progress. They were constantly being shoved and jostled as they bulldozed their way through the crowd, but there wasn't time to explain the reason for their urgency.

When they were getting quite close, someone barged into Sienna, knocking her to the ground, but Sophie knew she couldn't stop to help her up. She could see the assassin approaching the Prime Minister and in a few seconds she could be too late.

Unaware of the drama that was about to unfold, the

Prime Minister was chatting to an elderly man who was proudly wearing a row of medals on the front of his blazer. He shook the man's hand and thanked him for the service he had given his country, then turned towards the man in the green jacket and offered his hand in greeting.

'Hello,' he said, 'how nice to meet you.'

But when the man in the green jacket took his hand out of his pocket, instead of shaking the Prime Minister's hand he was holding a small gun.

'No, not hello, Prime Minister,' he said. 'This is where you say goodbye.'

Summoning up her last reserves of energy, Sophie launched herself through the air and slammed the sole of her borrowed boot into the assassin's chest, knocking him forcefully to the ground and sending the gun scudding across the cobblestones to land at the feet of Will Starkey.

For a few seconds there was pandemonium in the square, then a massive scrum ensued as the Prime Minister's security staff leapt on top of the man, pinning him to the floor so they could restrain and handcuff him. By the time Sienna arrived on the scene, the assassin was face down on the ground with a very large security man kneeling on his back.

The Prime Minister was determined to stay calm. He was aware that what he did next would be headline news all over the world, and he knew he should choose his words very carefully. He helped Sophie to her feet and thanked her for her decisiveness and courage, then invited her to accompany him on the rest of his walkabout to show the world that the British people will not be cowed by terrorists.

As the photographers swarmed around her, the realization of what she had just done hit Sophie like a thunderbolt. Cameras clicked and flashed, and the hoard of assembled journalists shouted out a barrage of questions, desperately trying to find out who she was. It was quite a shock and Sophie found it all a bit overwhelming.

Mrs Watson appeared at her side, looking ashen faced and a little shaken.

'Sophie darling,' she said, hugging her daughter close to her. 'Are you alright? What's this all about?'

'It's about bravery and patriotism,' said the Prime Minister, as the reporters jotted down every word.

'And look,' he continued, 'this brave girl seems to be the daughter of one of the local candidates standing for election. She obviously shares her mother's commitment to the democratic process.'

There was only one story on the national news that evening. A lone gunman had tried to assassinate the Prime Minister but was saved by the quick thinking and bravery of the daughter of local Green Party candidate Michelle Watson. Within a few hours Sophie and Mrs Watson were known all over the world and the press were clamouring for interviews. It was difficult to take it all in.

When Sophie woke up the following morning, she was horrified when she saw how many photographers and reporters had gathered outside their house. There were dozens of cameras trained on the Watson's front door, and a crowd of sightseers were already assembling on the other side of the road. She felt like drawing the curtains and going back to bed. All the newspaper front pages were full of Sophie's heroics. There were photographs of her standing by the Prime Minister's side and snippets of the interviews she had given the previous evening.

But The Daily Press was running a slightly different take on the story. Their front page carried a photograph of Will Starkey and it was proclaiming him as the nation's hero.

Under a banner headline of "Courageous Daily Press reporter foils gunman" was a photograph taken moments after the attack. The assassin was handcuffed on the ground with a huge security man sitting on top of him, and Starkey was standing over them holding the gun he had just picked up from between his feet. He looked as if he had carried out a citizen's arrest. Sophie burst out laughing when she first saw the front page but her mum and dad were absolutely furious.

'How can they be so brazen,' Mrs Watson shouted. 'The other journalists were all there, they saw what happened. He can't possibly expect people to believe all that nonsense.'

But when they turned on the television they were even more shocked. Breakfast with Kerry and Dane had a special guest dropping in for a chat, none other than 'the hero of the hour' Will Starkey. Mrs Watson just stood and stared at the TV screen in amazement.

'He's not seriously going to go on TV and repeat all that rubbish is he?' she said, unable to believe what was happening.

But when the show returned after the commercial break, Will Starkey was sitting on the sofa looking as if he had just won the lottery. He was leaning back with a smug smile plastered across his face, soaking up every glorious moment.

'But weren't you frightened at all?' Kerry asked. 'I mean, that gunman came out of nowhere.'

'Well, that's where my time in the Territorial Army stood me in good stead,' said Starkey. 'I knew there was no time for fear. I had to take decisive action.'

'Take what decisive action?' Mrs Watson screamed. 'Bend down to pick up a gun, then stand there looking gormless.'

She was pacing around the room looking as if she was about to explode.

'Of course, I was fortunate that the young girl distracted him for a moment,' Starkey continued, 'but once you've been trained for this kind of combat situation, courage becomes second nature. You just have to be in the moment and act instinctively.'

'I'll strangle him when I get my hands on him,' Mrs Watson shouted.

'Not if I get there first,' said Mr Watson.

Sophie wasn't at all put out by Starkey's claims. She didn't enjoy being in the limelight and anything that could distract the press from what she was doing was alright by her. She thought Starkey cut a pathetic figure, sitting on the sofa looking for validation from other people. It looked like such an empty existence.

'Are those newspaper people going to be outside the house all day?' she said, as her mum piled a load of paperwork into her bag.

Mrs Watson looked out of the window at the assembled crowd.

'I suppose it would be good if we could get them to leave us alone for the rest of the day,' she said. 'Perhaps we should do a deal with them. We'll answer a few questions and pose for photos on the doorstep, and in return they leave us alone until after tonight's election. What do you think?'

Sophie had no desire to answer any more stupid questions, but the thought of getting rid of the crowd for the rest of the day was far too tempting. She smiled for the camera, answered lots of stupid questions and smiled again, and soon the crowd of newspaper people had left them in peace.

A short time later the girls had the house to themselves. It was the day of the election and Mrs Watson had a busy day ahead of her at the Green Party headquarters in the town. There were a multitude of phone calls to be made, and Mr Watson had agreed to ferry some elderly people to and from the polling station. They were determined to fight for every vote they could get.

When Sophie returned to the living room after seeing her parents off, she was looking forward to a relaxed and crisis free morning. The events of the last twenty four hours had pushed her to the limit and she was hoping today would be a little more sedate. But Sienna seemed to have different ideas. She was looking at the letter she had taken from Professor Felso's study and it didn't look like she planned to do much sitting around.

'So, how far away would you say this apartment is?' she said, looking to get quickly back to her search.

'Erm, it's in the old town,' said Sophie, 'about twenty minutes away on foot. Perhaps we could go over there this afternoon.'

'Why wait until this afternoon?' said Sienna. 'If this is where Osorio is, let's get to him before he disappears into the woodwork again.'

Sophie's heart sank. She didn't want to start another argument, but it would have been nice to spend a few hours with Sienna without worrying that their lives were in imminent danger. She stared out the window looking for inspiration and was horrified to see there were still two newspaper reporters standing outside the garden gate. So much for the agreement they had made.

She was even more annoyed when one of them

opened the gate and began walking down the path towards the house. And then she suddenly realised. They weren't newspaper reporters at all. They were Osorio's guards and they would soon be at her front door.

She gasped in horror and backed away from the window.

'Oh no,' she said, putting her hands up to her face. 'Please no, not here.'

CHAPTER 19

The shock of seeing Osorio's guards approaching her house sent Sophie into a total panic. She stood there, frozen to the spot, unable to believe her home was about to be invaded. When Sienna grabbed her by the arm and started dragging her towards the rear of the house she was still in a bit of a haze.

'Is there a back gate at the end of the garden?' said Sienna, pulling open the kitchen door.

It took Sophie a few seconds to answer.

'Sophie!' Sienna shouted. 'Is there a back way out?'

'Erm, yes,' Sophie mumbled, 'well actually no. The garden backs onto the garden of the house opposite us. We're totally hemmed in.'

By now the girls were standing on the patio outside the kitchen and they could hear the guards banging heavily on the front door. Sienna dragged Sophie towards the end of the garden, took a quick look over the fence, then bent down and cupped her hands.

'Put your foot in here,' she said. 'I'll hoist you over.'

Sophie hesitated.

'But that's someone else's garden.'

'Sophie, this is no time for politeness. I'll give it ten seconds and they'll be at the back of the house.'

Sophie put her foot into Sienna's cupped hands and was immediately hoisted up and over the fence. She clattered to the ground on the other side and by the time she had managed to get to her feet Sienna had already joined her. Further up the garden, an elderly couple were tending to some plants in the window boxes outside their kitchen. They didn't see the girls until they were only a few feet away from them.

'So sorry to trouble you,' said Sophie as they ran past. She wanted to add some sort of explanation for the girls' sudden appearance but every idea she thought of sounded utterly ridiculous.

They bolted down the side of the house and out into the street, then crossed the road and made for the little park that was a bit further down. Once they'd managed to find a quiet spot behind the cover of some bushes, they crouched down and tried to catch their breath.

'Well, it didn't take him long to find us, did it?' said Sienna.

'Hardly surprising,' Sophie answered. 'If the newspapers know where we live, it wouldn't take much effort for Osorio to work it out.'

But Sophie knew it didn't matter how he'd found the address. The important thing was that Osorio now knew where she lived and from this moment on she and Sienna were in this together. And they would be until Sienna was successful in her quest.

Sienna took out the letter they had found on Professor Felso's desk.

'So,' she said. 'Shall we take a look at that apartment block?'

Sophie nodded, slowly realising that her life had just changed forever.

They set off for the other side of town, keeping a watchful eye out for any sign of the guards. Osorio was looking for the girls and the girls were looking for Osorio. It was only a matter of time before they met up again.

The apartment building was in the old part of the town, a popular location at weekends because of its fashionable cafes and bars. The Watsons had enjoyed a few long lazy lunches there on Sundays, and several local celebrities had recently bought property in the area.

It didn't take long to find the building. It was a converted four storey warehouse that had been launched in a fanfare of publicity about six months ago and stood out like a trophy building amongst the shabby chic of its surroundings. They ducked into a café on the opposite side of the road and sat by the window observing the comings and goings. It was still only mid-morning and the area hadn't really come to life. This was where the night owls lived.

After a while Sienna sensed some movement at the top of the building, and when she cast her gaze up to the roof she found what she was looking for. It was Osorio. He was out on a roof terrace speaking into a phone. He seemed angry and was barking instructions at someone. Sienna tapped Sophie on the arm and pointed up to the roof.

'So what do we do now?' Sophie asked.

'Let's wait and see what he does,' Sienna answered.

They didn't have to wait long. Within a few minutes Osorio burst through the front door of the building and walked aggressively towards a waiting car. As soon as he was inside, the car sped off. It all happened in a matter of seconds.

'This is our chance,' said Sienna. 'We've got to get inside that apartment and find out what his plans are.'

'But how?' said Sophie. 'This is quite an expensive building. There'll be a doorman and security locks. We can't just walk in.'

'We'll find a way,' said Sienna. 'There's always a way.'

Sophie thought about it for a few moments.

'We should go around to the other side of the building,' she said. 'These apartments are worth a fortune so there must be a secure parking area. If there is, then there'll be a rear entrance.'

'Excellent,' said Sienna. 'Let's go and take a look.'

They had to walk quite a way before they found the service road that led to the rear of the building, but it was worth the walk. There were allotted parking spaces for each of the apartments and, more importantly, there was an old style metal fire escape that ran up the outside of the apartment block. It was totally enclosed in a metal frame and the entrance was blocked by a security gate, but that wasn't going to deter Sienna.

'We could climb up the outside framework of the fire escape until we reach that gap just above the first floor,' she said, sounding excited. 'I think we could just about squeeze through there.'

Sophie wasn't so sure.

'But we'd be in full view of everyone in the surrounding properties,' she said. 'We're bound to be spotted.'

'Not if we're quick,' said Sienna.

Sophie knew it was useless arguing with Sienna and that sooner or later she would agree to do it, so she followed her to the bottom of the fire escape and started climbing up the metal framework. Spits and spots of rain were starting to fall and at times it was hard to get a proper grip on the slippery metal surface. When they reached the gap they had spotted, it looked slightly larger than it had from the ground. Sienna scrambled inside then turned to help Sophie through. As she did, she spotted a car moving towards them a little further down the service road.

'You'd better make it quick, Sophie,' she said, 'there's a car coming.'

She half helped, half dragged Sophie through the gap and soon they were both safely cocooned inside the fire escape. From there it was a simple journey to the top level.

The roof terrace was quite extensive and offered fabulous views across the old town. There were pot plants and garden furniture and a free standing barbecue that had obviously seen a lot of use during the summer months. Sophie could feel the nerves bubbling away inside her. Walking into Osorio's headquarters was such a massive risk, but she knew there could be no turning back now. She just hoped they could get this over with quickly and be on their way before Osorio returned.

A large sliding door led to the apartment. When Sienna tugged at the handle she expected it to be securely locked, but to her surprise it slid smoothly open revealing the plush interior of the apartment.

'Looks like we're in luck,' she said, turning back towards Sophie.

The look on Sophie's face told a different story though. She was staring right past Sienna, wide-eyed in terror, and when Sienna turned to step into the apartment she understood why. It was Osorio. He was standing a few feet in front of her and he was pointing a gun at her head.

CHAPTER 20

'You just won't give up, will you?' said Osorio, narrowing his eyes, menacingly.

Sienna gasped and quickly backed away from the door, scanning the floor for any makeshift weapons she could pick up.

'Get back over there with your friend,' Osorio barked.

'Or what?' Sienna shouted. 'Or you'll shoot? I don't think so. We're in full view of the surrounding properties and that shot would be heard for miles.'

'We've come for The Orb,' said Sophie, stepping forward, 'and we're not leaving without it.'

As Osorio turned to face Sophie, Sienna saw her opportunity. She leapt forward, clattering into Osorio, knocking him backwards into a collection of giant pot plants. He fell to the floor heavily and as his arm folded under him, his grip on the gun loosened and it skittered across the floor, just out of his reach.

As they wrestled amongst the foliage, Sophie rushed over to grab the gun but, when she turned back to help Sienna, Osorio had already gained the upper hand. He yanked Sienna to her feet, twisting her arm up behind her back, and dragged her over to the edge of the roof terrace.

'Give me the gun or your friend goes over the side,' he shouted.

Sophie was frozen with terror. She pointed the gun at Osorio's head but she didn't know whether she could actually pull the trigger.

'I won't tell you again,' Osorio shouted, moving Sienna nearer to the edge. 'Put the gun down on the ground and walk away from it.'

Sienna was shocked at how powerful Osorio was. When she struggled with him on the cliff top on Kestrel Island she felt like they were evenly matched, but on this occasion he had overpowered her fairly easily. He didn't even seem to be breathing heavily.

'Don't give him the gun, Sophie,' she shouted, trying desperately to fight back. 'If he does what he's threatening to do, shoot him.'

Sophie could see her hands shaking. Osorio was using Sienna as a human shield and, even though his head was still visible, she wasn't sure whether she could risk taking a shot at him.

'I'll count to five,' Osorio shouted. 'This is your last chance. One, two……'

Sophie was in a panic. She knew she couldn't hand over the gun, but she was terrified that Osorio would follow through on his threat.

'Three, four……'

Sophie swallowed hard and held her breath.

'Five!'

Everything seemed to stand still for a few seconds. It was the moment of truth. Then Osorio pulled Sienna's arm even further up her back and, as she gasped in pain, he spun her around and flipped her over the side of the building.

'No!' Sophie shouted, as she watched her friend disappear over the edge. She wanted to fire the gun and splatter Osorio all over the old town, but something was stopping her from pulling the trigger. Osorio slowly advanced on her, grim faced and unblinking. He seemed to ooze menace and evil.

'You won't pull that trigger,' he said. 'It takes a

certain kind of person to end another life and you're not that person.'

She wanted to do it. Osorio had just killed her friend, thrown her off a four storey building, and Sophie wanted to totally obliterate him. What was stopping her? Why couldn't she do it? She backed away from him still training the gun at his head.

One floor down, Sienna was clinging to one of the support poles on the outside framework of the fire escape, desperately hanging on for dear life. It was a stroke of good fortune that she was face down when she was falling and had seen the opportunity to grab hold of something, but she was still in a perilous position. Her grip on the slippery surface of the pole was slowly starting to weaken and she couldn't find a secure foothold anywhere. She tried, once again, to hook her foot into a bracket that held a drainpipe onto the wall, determined to get back up to that roof terrace. This couldn't be how it all ended. She was so close to victory.

Osorio was getting closer. Sophie could feel her whole body shaking. Her finger seemed frozen on the trigger of the gun, unable to exert any more pressure. But when Osorio leapt at her something snapped inside her head and she fired the gun at him at point blank range.

For some reason it didn't stop him from coming forward. In fact, if she hadn't stepped slightly to one side he would have slammed right into her. As it was they collided heavily, and when they spun apart they both went crashing to the ground.

Sophie jumped to her feet and backed away, still holding onto the gun. As she did, Osorio eyed her maliciously and slowly stood up. He didn't even seem to be wounded. She must have missed him. As he advanced on her again, she backed away, desperately trying to think of what to do.

'You won't win, you know,' said Osorio. 'I'm too powerful for you. It's only a matter of time before I send you down to join your friend.'

'Not if I have anything to do with it,' said Sienna, climbing back onto the roof.

Osorio was so shocked to see Sienna back on the roof terrace that he seemed to momentarily lose his mind. He charged at her impetuously, intent on finishing this once and for all. But just as he was about to smash into her, Sienna stepped to one side and in an effort to halt his momentum Osorio stumbled awkwardly and plummeted over the edge of the building. When the girls rushed forward to look over the side, his prone body was splattered on the concrete forty feet below them.

Sienna knew she had to get to the ground before anyone managed to discover the body. She hurtled down the fire escape, her eyes wide in anticipation, and burst through the security door onto the road. Finally, after months of having to deal with the disappointment of Kestrel Island, she was about to reclaim The Orb for her people. She could return home to Galacdros in triumph.

There was nobody around. The road was totally deserted. She knelt over Osorio's broken body and started urgently going through his pockets trying to find the precious artefact. But she couldn't find it anywhere. When Sophie arrived Sienna looked up at her in confusion.

'It's not here,' she said.

'Are you sure?' said Sophie.

Sienna searched again but still couldn't find The Orb. She turned out every pocket. They were all empty. And then she saw the fracture in his neck and the small wires poking out of it. This wasn't Osorio at all. It was another android.

When Sophie saw the wires, everything began to make sense to her. The way Osorio was easily able to overpower Sienna. The shot she fired that didn't stop him from moving towards her. The fact that he was still at the apartment when they had just seen him leaving through the front door.

'This must be what Professor Felso was talking about when he was trying to warn us about other androids,' she said.

Sienna didn't respond. Her disappointment was overwhelming. She just sat there staring blankly ahead, as if all the energy had drained out of her.

'We need to get away from here before someone discovers us with the body,' said Sophie.

She tried to drag Sienna to her feet and guide her away from the lifeless figure of the android, but Sienna seemed reluctant to leave. She was devastated. Her warrior spirit had completely deserted her.

'Come on, Sienna,' said Sophie, pulling at her again. 'We've got to get out of here.'

Her fears were confirmed when two of Osorio's guards appeared at the far end of the road and started charging towards them at lightning speed. What was she to do now? There was only one way in or out of the service road and the girls were totally surrounded by tall buildings. Fortunately, the sight of the guards seemed to bring Sienna crashing back to reality.

'Back this way,' she shouted. 'There might be an open door in one of these buildings down at the end.'

They grabbed frantically at the doors of every building but they were all securely locked. Sienna knew it was only a matter of time before Osorio appeared on the scene. She looked around for inspiration, her heart pounding in her chest, desperately trying to think of a way out.

Then a car appeared at the top of the road, turned on all its lights and started driving at speed in their direction. It was moving much too fast for such a small side road, and as it approached the guards it swerved at the last minute and tried to smash into both of them. They dived out of the way and rolled amongst the debris and the bins as the car hurtled on towards Sophie and Sienna.

It appeared to be heading straight at the girls, showing no signs at all of slowing down. Then just as Sophie thought it was going to plough right into them, it suddenly slammed on the brakes and, in a cacophony of screeching and spinning wheels, it pivoted on the spot and spun around to point back in the direction it had come from. As it did, the rear door flew open.

'Get in!' shouted a voice.

Sienna didn't need to be asked twice. She grabbed hold of Sophie, pushed her headlong through the open door then dived in after her. With the door still flapping open, the car set off again at high speed. As it passed the guards Sophie could hear bullets bouncing off the side of the car but she kept her head down, praying their luck would hold, still unsure who could have known they were so desperately in need of help.

CHAPTER 21

Once they reached the main road Sophie lifted her head and looked across at the driver, but the sight she was greeted with was a total surprise. It was an elderly lady with a feather sticking out of her hat and she was driving the car like a character from Grand Theft Auto. She seemed very calm, despite the bullet holes in the windscreen. It was all very strange.

Further down the road, the car pulled into a service station and sped down a ramp into the basement. As it came to a halt the driver turned and looked over her shoulder.

'Is everyone OK back there?' she asked. She was acting as if they had just been on a pony ride around the garden.

Sienna slumped back in her seat. She was massively relieved to have escaped the guards but still devastated not to have re-taken The Orb.

'How did you know we were there?' she asked.

'We've been watching that apartment for the last two days,' said the driver, 'so when you turned up this morning we were already in position.'

She glanced across at Sophie and smiled warmly.

'Hello Sophie,' she said, 'my name is Jutan. I'm a friend of Sienna's father.'

'Oh hello,' said Sophie, still trying to take everything in.

'I thought we'd got him,' said Sienna, shaking her head despondently. 'Osorio fell off the roof terrace and I thought I was about to reclaim The Orb but, when we got to the ground and searched him, it wasn't Osorio at all. It was just an android.'

'So he found Professor Felso,' said Jutan, looking a little concerned. 'That's not very good news.'

'Yes, he did,' Sienna replied, 'but fortunately, the professor realised his mistake and changed sides before it was too late.'

She updated Jutan on everything that had occurred during the terrifying hours they spent in the tunnels, including Felso's decision to slow down production of the androids and his brave attempt to grab The Orb.

'I'm afraid his body is still in those tunnels

somewhere,' said Sophie. 'We tried to save him but there was nothing more we could do.'

'You've both achieved a tremendous amount,' Jutan replied, 'Osorio is much weaker because of your efforts.'

'But he still has The Orb,' said Sienna. 'I thought we'd defeated him at the apartment, but once again I've been left empty handed.'

'Don't be too downhearted,' said Jutan, 'your chance will come again. But you will both need to be vigilant from now on. We believe powerful forces were behind that plot to kill the Prime Minister and they will undoubtedly be looking to take their revenge.'

'Who are these powerful forces?' Sophie asked.

'Well, Osorio is definitely one of them,' Jutan answered, 'but he is only one piece of the jigsaw. The driving force is thought to be a powerful businessman called James Masterson, and there are others in the group who are equally ruthless and ambitious. All of them believe they were born to rule and feel it is their right to take whatever they want. They are hungry for power and will not be pleased that the assassination attempt was unsuccessful.'

'But I thought Osorio was intent on seizing power in Galacdros,' said Sienna.

'He is,' said Jutan, 'but we think he's trying to build a power base in this world first so he'll be in a stronger position when he makes his move.'

They talked for over an hour and once again Jutan warned the girls to be on their guard in the coming days and weeks.

'You have disrupted the plans of a very dangerous group of people,' she said, 'and they will be determined to make sure you don't get away with it. My advice to you is to keep out of sight for the next few days and let the fire of their anger die down.'

They crossed the road and climbed into a less battle damaged car, then Jutan drove the girls back across the town, dropping them off just around the corner from Sophie's house. As they parted company, she warned them to approach the house with caution now that Osorio knows where they live, but she needn't have worried. There were two police cars sitting right outside the front gate and the local locksmith was parked a little further down.

'Oh, thank heavens you're alright,' said Mrs Watson, when she saw Sophie and Sienna walking up the garden path. 'I wondered where you were. You weren't answering any of my calls or texts.'

'Sorry Mum,' said Sophie, 'but I'm afraid I've lost my phone somewhere. What happened here?'

'Looks like a forced entry madam,' said the young police officer who was standing nearby. 'It was quite a bold thing to do, just break in through the front door. You don't often see that in a nice area like this.'

When Sophie saw the inside of the house she was shocked by the level of destruction. It looked like it had been hit by a hurricane.

'They've completely ransacked the place,' said Mrs Watson, 'but they don't seem to have taken very much. The TV and computer are still intact and they haven't touched any of my jewellery.'

An older policeman in a suit appeared from the kitchen, looking a little concerned. He had been speaking to someone on the phone and as he approached Mrs Watson he hung up.

'I don't think it would be safe for you and your family to stay here for the time being, Mrs Watson,' he said. 'Whoever did this was obviously intent on causing harm and they may not stop until someone has been seriously hurt.'

'But where can we go?' she asked.

'We've reserved some rooms for you at The Queen's

Hotel on Market Square,' he said. 'We'd like you to stay there until after the election. We can post a couple of plain clothes officers in the lobby, and you'll only have a short walk across the square to hear the election result at the town hall.'

'So you don't think this was just another burglary then.'

'I'm afraid not,' he answered. 'This doesn't look like the work of your average criminal. There's something quite strange about this break-in, something that's making me feel very uncomfortable.'

In a different hotel, in the old part of the town, Will Starkey was on the phone to his editor.

'The whole country is waiting to see what you come up with next Will,' she told him. 'So go out there and dig up another story. Sniff around. Find someone doing something they shouldn't. Make it really juicy and you'll be on the front page again tomorrow.'

And Starkey liked being on the front page. When he bent down and picked up that gun from between his feet the previous day, he had no idea he was about to become headline news. The photograph certainly gave the impression that he had just saved the day and when his editor saw it she was determined to make it their lead story.

'The whole world loves a hero, Will,' she said, 'and today that hero is you.'

Starkey didn't even hesitate. He had been in the newspaper business long enough to know that it's not the truth that sells newspapers, it's the story. And right now he was the story. The Daily Press was the biggest selling newspaper in the country, and in the eyes of its readers Will Starkey was now a national hero.

CHAPTER 22

By the time evening arrived, the Watsons and Sienna had checked into The Queen's Hotel and were eagerly awaiting the announcement of the election result later that night. Sophie's mum had set up an office in one of the small rooms on the top floor and her dad was making sure he was at his wife's side at all times. He was convinced the break-in had something to do with the election and he wasn't prepared to let Mrs Watson out of his sight.

Sophie and Sienna sat in Sophie's room, overlooking the square, chatting about the events of the last two days and speculating on what they thought Osorio might try next.

'I hope he's not planning to interfere with the election,' said Sophie. 'Mum has worked so hard in the last few weeks. She deserves to get a good result tonight.'

'Well, I'm sure your heroics yesterday afternoon won't have done her any harm,' said Sienna, smiling at her.

Sophie walked over to the window and stared down at the square. It was bustling with noise and excitement as the night revellers moved raucously around, laughing and jostling each other while making their way off into the shadows. A man was singing in a tuneless voice, supported by two friends, one on either side. Whatever it was he was celebrating, he had obviously started much earlier that evening.

At the far side of the square, Will Starkey appeared on the steps of the town hall. He scrawled something onto a notepad then stuffed it into his pocket and trudged wearily down the steps into the night. Dodging down the side of the town hall, he looked for a spot in the shadows where he could gather his thoughts for a few moments, but he soon realised he was not alone. In a dimly lit area a little further down, someone was moving boxes around close to two white vans. He decided to edge a little closer to find out what was going on.

Sophie watched him as he skulked around, creeping in and out of the shadows. Why was he acting so suspiciously? She turned to Sienna, who was stretched out on the bed staring up at the ceiling.

'I can see Will Starkey,' she said, 'and as usual it looks like he's up to no good.'

Sienna sprang to her feet and joined Sophie by the window.

'He looks as if he's spying on someone,' she said. 'I wonder what he's doing.'

'I'd love to go down there and make him justify what he said on TV this morning,' said Sophie.

'Why don't we?' Sienna answered.

A smile broke out on Sophie's face.

'It would be fun to freak him out, wouldn't it?'

It felt good to be out in the cool night air having been stuck in a tiny hotel room for most of the evening. As they strolled across the square, heading towards the town hall, Sophie still couldn't believe the outrageous claims Starkey had made on television that morning, particularly when so many people witnessed what had actually happened. She was really looking forward to confronting him about it.

Further down in the shadows, Starkey had ducked behind a parked car and was monitoring what was taking place between the two white vans. He watched for a couple of minutes as a man loaded black boxes into one of the vans then took identical boxes out and put them in the vehicle parked alongside. There was no mistaking what the large white letters on the side of the boxes said. Ballot Box. Could he have stumbled upon a vote rigging scandal?

The excitement rose up inside him. This could be the story he had been looking for. He took out his phone and started to video what the man was doing, already visualising his story plastered across the front page of The Daily Press. But within seconds he felt something hard poke into the small of his back, and a voice from behind him spoke calmly and with menace.

'Don't turn around,' a man said. 'Just walk calmly over to those vans and don't say a word.'

A hand came over Starkey's shoulder and took the phone from him then pushed him aggressively in the direction of the vans. It threw him into a panic. If that really was a gun poking into his back, this wasn't the kind of story he had been looking to find.

When they reached the vans, the face of the man who was loading and unloading boxes looked very familiar. He was so similar in appearance to the gunman from the previous day that they had to be brothers. Then the man who had accosted him and taken his phone stepped to one side and Starkey realized that he also looked identical to the assassin. What was going on?

As he struggled to make sense of it all, he noticed some movement a little further up towards Market Square. Two figures were walking slowly down towards them and it wasn't long before he realized who they were. It was that Watson girl who had thwarted the assassination attempt yesterday afternoon, and she was with her aggressive friend. Should he do something to try to warn them? No, that could be fatal. It was much better to concentrate on getting himself out of trouble. The girls could worry about themselves.

The man with the gun grabbed Starkey by the shoulder.

'Stay here by the van and act natural,' he said, poking the gun into Starkey's ribs. Then the two men darted behind one of the vans leaving Starkey to deal with the situation.

As the girls approached him, Sophie thought Starkey looked genuinely terrified by the prospect of meeting her again, as if he knew what he had said on TV that morning was totally wrong and he was about to get his comeuppance. She smiled at him mockingly.

'Well, well,' she said. 'It's the man who saved the Prime Minister's life.'

But before Starkey could answer her, one of the guards stepped out from behind the van and pointed his gun at Sophie's head. He still had that weird smile on his face but the girls knew that this was no laughing matter.

'OK,' said the guard, 'we're all going to get into the back of this van. Any sudden movements and it will be your last.'

He forced them into the van and made them lie on the floor face down, then climbed in after them and pulled the doors shut. Starkey could now see quite clearly that the boxes they were lying alongside were ballot boxes. He may have stumbled upon the story his editor was looking for but now it looked like he would never get a chance to write it.

The other guard jumped into the driver's seat and the van pulled away from the town hall and sped off into the night. After driving through the streets of Hampton Spa for a few minutes, they turned into a side street, bumped along some cobblestones then came to a halt.

'OK,' said the guard. 'When I open the door we're going to get out of the van and walk calmly down the steps into the basement. If anyone tries to be a hero they'll be making a big mistake.' Then he pushed open the back door and climbed out.

As soon as Sophie stepped out into the street she knew exactly where she was. They were standing by the steps the android Sienna had lured her down the previous day. She shuddered at the thought of it. In the dim light thrown out by a lone street lamp, anyone driving past would never have noticed the small gun the guard was holding against Sienna's back as he marched the three of them down the steps into the basement. As he did, the van sped away leaving the area in darkness.

'Get over there by the wall,' said the guard, pushing the door shut behind him.

He took out his phone and pushed a number on speed dial. Within seconds a voice answered that Sophie and Sienna recognized immediately.

'Yes, what is it?' said Osorio.

'The mission has been accomplished,' said the guard.

'Excellent,' Osorio answered.

'And I have a bonus for you as well,' said the guard. 'I've found those girls you've been looking for, and also that newspaper man who helped to save the Prime Minister. I have all three of them down here in the basement.'

Osorio didn't answer. The silence was unbearable.

'What shall I do with them?' the guard asked.

There was another slight pause.

'Kill them,' said Osorio. Then he hung up.

CHAPTER 23

On hearing Osorio's words, Starkey began to get hysterical. The calm military mind he had spoken so boastfully about when he was on breakfast TV earlier that day was nowhere to be seen.

'Please,' he said. 'I had nothing to do with saving the Prime Minister's life. It was my editor's idea. She made the whole thing up.'

He turned to the girls.

'Tell him, please, this has nothing to do with me.'

Sophie knew they had to do something, and quickly. The guard was just a machine. He had been given his orders and now he was likely to carry them out without delay. They may only have a few seconds left to live.

There was a thick wooden pole lying on the ground that would make a great weapon. If she could cause a massive disturbance and distract the guard's attention, perhaps it would create enough time for Sienna to grab the pole and launch an attack. She tried to focus her mind to send Sienna a telepathic message, warning her that she was about to cause a diversion. She just hoped Sienna would be ready when she made her move.

Starkey was still desperately pleading with the guard. He was starting to shake and he looked as if he was about to cry. He turned towards Sophie, looking like a helpless lamb on its way to slaughter.

'Please tell him,' he pleaded. 'Tell him it was nothing to do with me.'

It was now or never. Sophie knew she had to take action.

'Oh why don't you stop whining!' she screamed at him. 'Be a man for once in your life.'

She stepped forward to where Starkey stood pleading and begging for his life, drew back her arm and punched him hard in the face. It was such an unexpected turn of events that it took everyone completely by surprise. Starkey cried out in pain and stumbled backwards, causing the guard to jump out of the way to avoid being involved in a collision.

In the brief moment of confusion that followed, Sienna grabbed the wooden pole from the ground and, summoning up all her power, smashed it down onto the guard's head. He staggered back and rocked on his feet for a second, but then he seemed to be gathering himself again. She slammed the pole into his skull again and again, and as he slumped back against the wall she grabbed the gun that hung limply from his hand, jammed the barrel into his mouth and pulled the trigger. The bullet ripped upwards, straight into his circuit boards and within seconds smoke and a few sparks flashed from his open mouth. As he collapsed to the ground, fizzing and sparking, Sophie saw the chance for them to make their escape.

'Let's get out of here!' she shouted. 'His friend might be back any minute.'

She grabbed Starkey's arm and pulled him to his feet. He was wide-eyed and open-mouthed and looked as if he was still in shock. They had to drag him out of the basement and up the steps, and it wasn't until they were some distance away that they felt it was safe to stop running.

'What's going on here,' said Starkey, looking totally confused. 'Who were those people? And why did you attack me like that?'

'More importantly,' said Sienna, 'what were you

doing hanging around with them?'

'I wasn't hanging around with them,' he said. 'I saw them skulking around at the side of the town hall and went down to investigate. It looked as if they were messing around with some ballot boxes.'

'Ballot boxes?' said Sophie, looking a little alarmed. 'You don't think they were trying to rig the election, do you?'

'Well, that's what it looked like to me.'

'Oh no,' said Sophie. 'We've got to get back to the town hall and stop them from announcing that result. Mum's worked too hard to be cheated out of this at the last minute.'

She turned and charged back towards Market Square, running with a determination and strength she never realised was within her. Those long hours of training she had been doing since the end of the summer were finally starting to pay off. Matching her stride for stride, Sienna sprinted along beside her, but Starkey was hopelessly out of condition and the girls soon left him trailing far behind.

Powering through the streets of Hampton Spa, Sophie knew it was touch and go whether they would be able to make it back to the town hall in time. The result was due to be announced just after midnight, so they only had a few short minutes to get there. But she drove herself relentlessly forward. There was far too much at stake for them to fail.

By the time the girls reached Market Square, the last of the late night revellers were starting to make their weary way home. It may have been a cool and chilly night but Sophie was drenched with perspiration from the exertions of her dash across the town.

They rushed up the steps of the town hall with their hearts pounding in their chests and burst through the open door into the lobby. There was hardly anyone around, just a porter sitting behind a desk sifting through some paperwork in a plastic folder. Sophie rushed over to him.

'Excuse me,' she said, breathlessly. 'Could you tell me where the result of the election is due to be announced?'

'It's at the top of the stairs,' he said, 'in the Great Hall. But you'd better hurry. They've already started making the announcement.'

Tearing up the stairs, taking two steps at a time, they frantically searched around for the Great Hall. They could hear the sound of raucous cheering coming from a room at the far end of the corridor, followed by a woman making an announcement and a lot more shouting and cheering.

By the time they arrived in the Great Hall, they were so breathless they could hardly speak. There was a woman up on the stage talking into a microphone and when the cheering died down she stepped forward and spoke again.

'And as returning officer,' she said, 'I do hereby declare that Michelle Elizabeth Watson is duly elected as the Member of Parliament for Hampton Spa.'

Once again the crowd broke into a chorus of raucous shouting and cheering. Many of them were waving green flags and hugging one another. Still trying to catch her breath, Sophie watched with enormous pride as her mum stepped forward to make her acceptance speech, knowing that Hampton Spa couldn't be in safer hands.

It was a while before Sophie managed to get to her mum to congratulate her and give her a hug. There were swarms of people milling around and Mrs Watson was keen to thank everyone who had helped her during the campaign. She remained in the hall for some time, celebrating with her joyful supporters and chatting to the reporters who had stayed on to grab an interview.

As Sophie stood and watched her mum handshaking

her way around the room, Jutan appeared at her side, smiling broadly.

'That was an excellent result your mother achieved tonight, Sophie,' she said, 'but it could have been so much closer if you hadn't led us to those bogus ballot boxes.'

Sophie looked a little confused.

'But how did we help?' she asked.

'Well, I knew you wouldn't be able to stay cooped up in the hotel all evening, so I stationed one of our agents outside the door to follow you if you went outside. I was sure you'd lead us to whatever foul deed Osorio was planning, and so it turned out. I'm just sorry we didn't manage to get to you before you were taken away in that van, but once again you showed yourselves to be more than a match for Osorio.'

Having pushed themselves to the limit to get to the town hall in time, Sophie and Sienna decided to stroll out to the square to take advantage of the cool night air. They sat on a bench, watching supporters of the other political parties slowly making their way home to lick their wounds.

'So we didn't need to charge halfway across the town

after all,' said Sophie, with a big smile on her face. 'Mum won by such a big margin, those bogus ballot papers wouldn't have made any difference.'

'I suppose that's what comes from having a famous daughter,' said Sienna, smiling back at her.

'To be honest, I don't think I'm the famous type,' said Sophie. 'When I saw Will Starkey on TV this morning, soaking up all that publicity, I thought he looked a bit pathetic. I'm much happier just doing my own thing.'

They sat in silence for a moment. As they did, an image flashed into Sienna's head of her excitement as she was going through Osorio's pockets that morning. Finding out it was just an android had been a heavy blow to take.

'I wonder where Osorio is now,' she said, staring out across the square. 'I suppose I'll have to start looking for him all over again.'

'Either that or he'll find us,' said Sophie. 'One way or another I'm sure we're destined to encounter Osorio and his secret society again. There's no way they'll take this lying down.'

'This isn't your fight, Sophie,' said Sienna. 'You don't have to get involved in all of this.'

'I'm already involved,' said Sophie.

She thought about the guards who had come to her house that morning and the horror that would have ensued if she hadn't seen them coming.

'I realized everything had changed when I saw Osorio's guards walking down our garden path today,' she said. 'Now I intend to see this through to the bitter end. Osorio has already tried to kill us three times, and I don't want to spend the rest of my life looking over my shoulder. So I'm already involved. We're in this together.'

When the girls arrived back at the hotel, Sophie's mum and dad were already in the bar having a well-earned drink with some of Mrs Watson's closest supporters. This was a proud moment for Sophie and she was keen to join in the celebrations. Mr Watson ordered them a couple of long cold drinks and they raised their glasses and proposed a toast to the new MP for Hampton Spa.

They sat around a large table and chatted long into the night. Nobody wanted it all to end. Just as Sophie was thinking of moving up to bed a face appeared at the window. It was Will Starkey. He stopped for a moment and peered in at them then started to walk away. But at the last minute he turned and walked back towards the hotel entrance.

It was quite a surprise when he turned up at their table. He wasn't looking as arrogant and full of himself as he usually does and a large bruise was starting to develop on the side of his face. He nodded sheepishly to Mrs Watson.

'Congratulations,' he said. 'That was quite a victory you pulled off tonight.'

'Thank you,' said Mrs Watson. 'I suppose you'll be claiming the credit for it in tomorrow morning's paper, will you?'

Starkey didn't respond. For once he had to accept that he was totally in the wrong. Then he turned to face the girls.

'And thanks for your help earlier on,' he said. 'That wasn't exactly my finest hour, was it?'

'That's OK,' said Sienna. 'Once you've been trained for combat situations, courage becomes second nature.'

'Yes,' said Sophie. 'You just have to be in the moment and act instinctively.'

There was nothing Starkey could say. He just had to stand there and take it, then shuffle awkwardly back into the lobby.

'Well, I hope he goes home and takes a long hard look at himself in the mirror,' said Mrs Watson, as

Starkey made his way out of the hotel.

'Good idea, Mum,' said Sophie, smiling back at her. 'You never know. He might just spot that monster he's been looking for.'

Also by A.B. Martin

Raven's Wharf

It is mid-December and Sophie and Sienna find themselves on the wintry streets of London. Sienna is still hunting for her nemesis Osorio, and when they spot one of his henchmen near the home of the Prime Minister they realise Osorio can't be far away.

During a series of desperate chases and perilous escapes, they discover a dark secret that a powerful politician would like to keep hidden.

But could this discovery have deadly consequences? Secrets can be fatal, and now the girls know too much they'll be lucky to escape with their lives.

Raven's Wharf is a thrilling adventure story filled with breathtaking action, evil villains and courage in the face of adversity. It's an uplifting testament to the enduring power of friendship.

If you enjoyed this book…

Thank you so much for checking out Sophie and Sienna's latest adventure.

If you enjoyed reading the book, I'd be very grateful if you could spend a minute posting a review on your favourite online bookstore. Even one short sentence would be very much appreciated.

Reviews make a real difference to authors. They help other readers get a feel for the book, and I'd also be very interested to hear your thoughts on the story.

Thank you for your help,

A.B. Martin

Acknowledgements

Many thanks to Roisin Heycock for her expert notes and meticulous edit. Also to Stuart Bache at Books Covered for the wonderful cover design.

And a massive thank you to my wife, Annie Burchell, for her inspiration, advice and detailed analysis of the manuscript. Without her continuous input this book would still be sitting on my hard drive.

About the author

A.B. Martin is an English author who writes thrilling middle-grade adventure stories and intriguing mysteries.

Before becoming an author, he wrote extensively for television and radio and performed comedy in a vast array of venues, including the world famous London Palladium.

Under Crook's Wood is the second book in the Sophie Watson Adventure Mystery series. It was published in October 2018.

Kestrel Island, the first in the series, was published in 2017.

He lives in London, England, with his wife and daughter.

Printed in Great Britain
by Amazon

11929501R00133